He Was So Good Looking
She Could Hardly Believe It . . .

Johnny Trent looked appraisingly at Azalee. "How old are you? Sixteen?"

Azalee nodded.

"Well, where I come from, sixteen is old enough for lots of things—marriage, sometimes, and dancing for sure," he said, holding out his hand to her. "Miss Azalee—"

"Yes," Azalee said. She felt two strong hands around her waist. He lifted her off the step, swung her into the air and onto the floor. They took three turns, and they were in the middle of the ballroom.

Her head was against Johnny Trent's chest, and she willingly let him pull her closer to him. Her heart pounded and her blood sang, and all she wanted to do was to go on dancing with him forever. *Don't let the music stop,* she prayed silently, *don't let the music stop.*

He pulled her closer to him, and his heart pounded as her body curved willingly to his. He heard and felt her sharp intake of breath. She was only sixteen, but Johnny Trent knew that he held a woman in his arms . . .

DAWN OF LOVE HISTORICAL ROMANCES for you to enjoy

Available from ARCHWAY paperbacks

Dawn of Love

RECKLESS HEART

Dee Austin

AN ARCHWAY PAPERBACK
Published by POCKET BOOKS • NEW YORK

AN ARCHWAY PAPERBACK *Original*

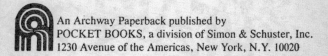

An Archway Paperback published by
POCKET BOOKS, a division of Simon & Schuster, Inc.
1230 Avenue of the Americas, New York, N.Y. 10020

ISBN: 0-671-55153-1

First Archway Paperback printing June, 1985

10 9 8 7 6 5 4 3 2 1

AN ARCHWAY PAPERBACK and colophon are
registered trademarks of Simon & Schuster, Inc.

DAWN OF LOVE is a registered trademark
of Bruck Communications, Inc.

Printed in the U.S.A.

IL 7+

RECKLESS HEART

Chapter 1

"AZIE, COME IN THIS INSTANT!"

Azalee La Fontaine pretended not to hear her grandmother. Well, it *was* hard to hear, what with the music and all. Dark-haired Azalee leaned even farther over the wrought-iron balcony, her long hair flowing in the wind. The regimental band was loud enough to drown out anybody's voice—even Grandmother Charlotte's.

"Azie!" Now her grandmother's gray head was close to her, and she could no longer pretend she didn't hear her.

"Yes, Nani Charlotte?"

"When are you going to remember that you're sixteen, not six? And a young lady of sixteen does not stand on a balcony wearing nothing more than a chemise. Inside!"

The green-eyed girl pulled her cashmere shawl more closely around her low-cut chemise, but her blossoming curves clung to the fabric of the shawl.

"Azalee!"

Azalee moved quickly through the glass doors into

her bedroom. When Nani Charlotte called her by her full name, she knew it was best to listen.

Her grandmother closed the doors to the balcony with a firm click. "When are you going to act your age?" she asked.

"If I'm so grown up," Azalee asked, "why can't I go to the regimental ball tonight?"

"Sixteen is too young to attend a ball. Seventeen is time for that. Your father is allowing you to go to the dinner before the ball, though in my day, that would have been unheard of for a girl of sixteen."

Azalee nodded. Although she seemed to be paying close attention to Grandmother Charlotte, her thoughts were far away. If only her mother had lived. Azalee was sure that the beautiful young woman whose picture smiled at her from the little table beside the bed would have been more understanding.

"Get dressed, Azie." Her grandmother's voice softened, as she, too, looked at the picture beside the bed. "I'll send Fanchon to help you. And try to remember that you're sixteen—a young lady."

Remember you're sixteen, Azie . . . act your age . . . grow up . . . Azalee sighed. When she was eleven and twelve and thirteen, she had thought that it would be wonderful to be sixteen. But now that she was, it seemed that she had traded the privileges of a child for a whole lot of rules, silly rules, for which she didn't care one bit.

Her grandmother paused at the bedroom door. "No more standing out half-naked on the balcony. Get dressed."

Azalee smiled and gave her grandmother a hug. "I'm sorry, Nani, but I heard the music from the Place d'Armes, and I was just trying to see—"

"You cannot see from here to the Place d'Armes," her grandmother said, "and it's just as well. If you could see the soldiers, then they could see you— wearing nothing but a chemise!"

"They're not just soldiers," Azalee said. "That was the band from our New Orleans Regiment. Everyone we know rides in that regiment—Gerard and Alain and—"

"And do you think it would be all right for Gerard and Alain Duval to see you without your clothes on? For the last time, Azie, get dressed!"

After her grandmother left, Azalee opened the door of the large oak cabinet that held the gown her father had brought her from Paris. She was just pulling the dress from its hanger when Fanchon came in. "No, Azie, not like that. Here. Let me do it."

Azalee stepped back. This exotic woman, who had come from Haiti to New Orleans with Azalee's mother, Isabella, and was beside the bed the day Isabella gave birth to Azalee, had stood in as Azalee's mother.

"Take care of my baby, Fanchon," Isabella had said, clutching Fanchon's hand. "Promise me."

Fanchon gave her word and, even when Pierre La Fontaine gave Fanchon her freedom, she did not go back to Haiti after Isabella died. A faithful friend, she stayed on in the La Fontaine household and cared for Azalee like a mother.

As she was growing up, Azalee asked Fanchon about her mother. "My Isabella," Fanchon would say, "she was the prettiest girl in Haiti and the prettiest girl in New Orleans. Maybe the prettiest girl in the whole world."

A ritual grew between them. Whenever Azalee would dress for a special occasion, she would ask Fanchon, "Am I as pretty as Isabella?"

The answer was always the same. "Pretty, yes, *chérie*. Prettiest girl in New Orleans. But as pretty as Isabella? No."

Now Azalee looked at her image in the mirror, as Fanchon fastened the row of pearls that served as buttons on her white organdy dress and tied the pale pink ribbon beneath the bodice. White dress, white silk slippers, and, before she left the house, her grandmother would make sure she was wearing white elbow-length kid gloves.

"White, white, white!" Azalee said, grumbling. "I feel like a pail of milk."

"Your grandmother is right," Fanchon said. "My *petite* is pretty in all white."

Azalee sighed and asked the expected question— was she as pretty as her mother? She knew what the answer would be. She didn't feel especially pretty. At that moment she would rather have been in her comfortable riding clothes than in the oh-so-ladylike white outfit.

Fanchon looked at her for what seemed like a long time. She saw Azalee and she remembered Isabella. Both were Creole beauties, a mixture of light and dark.

4

Their Spanish ancestors had bequeathed the dark hair, while their French side gave them camellia-white skin.

Isabella, Fanchon thought, *if only you were here to see your child. She has your beauty, and she has something more—a daring that sometimes makes me afraid for her.* She cleared her throat. "Perhaps even prettier," she finally said.

"Fanchon!" Azalee saw that there were tears in Fanchon's eyes. "Fanchon—"

"No," Fanchon said, holding her hands out to prevent Azalee from running to her, from hugging her. "You will crush the dress. Hurry. Your grandmother and your papa are waiting. It is time for you to go to the ball."

Azalee smiled, left the bedroom, and reminded herself not to run down the stairs—Nani Charlotte and Papa were watching. She remembered Fanchon's words. She was even prettier than her mother. Maybe it was time to try for Isabella's fine manners as well. "Forgive me if I kept you waiting," Azalee said.

Pierre La Fontaine looked at his daughter with surprise. Azalee walking down the stairs slowly and apologizing for keeping them waiting? What had gotten into her? Perhaps she was becoming a lady after all—a lady like Isabella.

Azalee's father shook his head. This was not the time to think about Isabella; the person he had to concentrate on was Azalee. And she needed his special attention. She might look like her mother, but the resemblance ended there. Isabella was shy and demure; she rarely raised those spectacular green eyes.

But Azalee! She was always looking about, eager and inquisitive. She wasn't the proper young lady that New Orleans society, even in this advanced age of 1814, was ready to accept.

Pierre helped his mother into the waiting carriage and then held out a hand to his daughter. It was a little after eight o'clock, and the street lamps flickered their yellow and blue flames over the balconies and homes that led the way to the grandest home of all—the Duval mansion.

It was going to be a wonderful evening; Azalee just knew it. It was true that, after the dinner, she and her friend Marguerite Brevard and some of the other young people would be sent upstairs, away from the dancing. But, at least she was allowed to attend the dinner, and, sitting in the grand dining room with her would be Alain Duval and his younger brother, Gerard.

It wasn't really fair, she decided, not fair at all. Alain and Gerard were her very good friends, but, because they were nineteen and seventeen, they were allowed to go to the ball, while she and Marguerite, who were only sixteen, were not.

Azalee smiled. Not that it mattered all that much. If she knew Alain and Gerard, they would dance one waltz with their mother or their captain's wife, and then they would hurry upstairs to where she and Marguerite would be waiting for them. Then the four of them would gossip about the other people at the ball, and Alain and Gerard would tell them amusing stories about what went on in the regiment. They wouldn't miss the silly dancing—not one bit!

When the La Fontaine carriage arrived at the Duval home, Azalee waited until her father handed her grandmother down from the carriage and then she held out her hand. Actually, she longed to jump from the carriage without help from anyone. It was so silly! She could jump off a horse without any trouble. Why did she have to pretend that she needed help taking two tiny steps from the carriage to the ground?

Still, Azalee forced herself to behave like a demure young lady. She knew it was what her father expected, and maybe, if she behaved properly, he would let her stay downstairs for the ball.

Monsieur Theodore and Madame Jeanne Duval were waiting to greet their guests, and, standing beside them were Gerard and Alain, each splendid in the short red jacket, white pants, and polished black boots that was the uniform of the New Orleans Regiment.

They were brothers, but they looked so different, Azalee thought to herself. Alain was taller and his hair was almost black, like hers. His square shoulders strained the fabric of his jacket, and his eyes were as dark as his hair. Gerard was an inch or two shorter than his brother, and his sandy-colored hair and gray eyes were in contrast to Alain's dark good looks.

Azalee curtseyed to Madame Duval, trying to avoid the amusement in Alain's eyes. Let him laugh at her demure behavior. Tonight she wanted Madame Duval to think of her as grown-up, certainly old enough to dance at the ball.

"Azalee," Madame Duval said, not one bit fooled by her downcast eyes and prim manner. "I hope you have a wonderful evening, my dear . . . within bounds, of course."

Within bounds. Azalee sighed. She knew what that meant. She could have a good time, but not *too* good a time, and she wasn't to do anything to upset anyone. "Thank you, Madame Duval," she whispered.

Pierre La Fontaine and Nani Charlotte were pleased with Azalee's behavior throughout dinner. She was seated with other young people and she didn't laugh too loudly or giggle. There was nothing they could object to.

It was close to ten-thirty when the dinner ended, and the musicians could be heard in the ballroom, tuning their instruments. Azalee looked pleadingly at her father and grandmother. Pierre La Fontaine turned his head away, but Nani Charlotte shook her head emphatically *no*. Azalee knew it was no use asking her grandmother if she could stay downstairs for the ball.

Matters were decided by Madame Duval, who approached the table of young people. "Azalee," she said, "Marguerite, Esmee, and Guilbert, you may be excused. I believe there is some lovely hot chocolate waiting for you upstairs in the nursery."

The nursery! Azalee was indignant. The nursery might be all right for Esmee and Guilbert—they were babies—but she and Marguerite belonged downstairs with Gerard, Alain, and the other young men of the New Orleans Regiment.

It just wasn't fair! Azalee was about to say that, even though Marguerite was pulling on her hand and whispering that it was really best not to make trouble. But it was Madame Duval who made her decide to say nothing. "Of course, Azalee," Madame Duval said, "if you would rather return home, I will understand. It is getting late and perhaps you would rather be in bed."

Azalee's face crimsoned. Sometimes she thought that Madame Duval was some kind of witch. She always seemed to know just what she was thinking. "Thank you, Madame Duval," Azalee said. "I'd rather stay here."

"Very well, my dear. Then please go upstairs with the others." Madame Duval seemed to take pity on Azalee then and softened. "It's only one more year, Azalee," she whispered. "You will be out in society next year, and there will be plenty of balls for you to go to then."

"Yes, Madame Duval," Azalee said, following Marguerite to the wide, curved staircase that led to the second floor of the house. "Thank you, Madame Duval." But inside she was seething. Fanchon had actually said she was prettier than Isabella, but she was still being sent upstairs. It was silly to have to wait for a whole year to be allowed to dance.

Alain and Gerard caught up with the girls at the bottom step. "Don't worry," Alain said, and he gave

Azalee's hand a squeeze. "Gerard and I will be upstairs as soon as we can get away."

Azalee's spirits lifted. "You'll come upstairs for a cup of hot chocolate, Alain?"

"I'll be up as soon as I can get away, Azie." He smiled, white teeth gleaming against his tanned skin. "You know I hate to be away from you."

"Alain!" said Marguerite, who had heard the short exchange. "You shouldn't speak that way!"

Azalee looked at her friend. Marguerite, with her blond ringlets and large blue eyes, looked and acted like such a baby. "Oh, Marguerite, you take everything so seriously! Come on, I'll race you to the nursery."

Marguerite walked up the stairs slowly, ignoring Azalee, who went flying by, her hoop skirts lifted, taking two steps at a time.

Pierre La Fontaine watched his daughter race up the stairs. He should scold her, he thought, but he didn't have the heart to do it.

"It's all right, sir." Alain Duval was standing by his side. "That's one of the things that makes Azie so special—she's so full of life. More than any other girl. It's one of the reasons we all love her."

Pierre La Fontaine looked at the tall dark-haired young man. It was clear that, when Alain said *all,* he really meant himself. But they were both so young—Azalee and Alain. Children. But not really children, Pierre La Fontaine reminded himself. Isabella was just seventeen when they had married, he just twenty-two. And that had been a different time, a slower time. With the war going on between the Americans and the British, time seemed to move much faster. Alain was only nineteen, but nineteen and a soldier. He was already a man.

"Sir," Alain said, "perhaps this is not the time to speak, perhaps it is even too soon—"

"You are right," Pierre La Fontaine dismissed him. He was brusque with this young man who wanted to take Azalee from him. "This is not the time, and it is too soon, far too soon. Azalee is only a child. Just a few moments ago your mother sent her upstairs to the nursery."

"Yes, sir." Alain looked so crushed that Pierre La Fontaine felt sorry for him.

"You're both young," Azalee's father said. "You have plenty of time, Alain. Wait a year, until Azalee is at least seventeen. We will talk then."

"Yes, sir," Alain said, looking toward the staircase and smiling. It was true that his mother had sent Azalee and Marguerite to the nursery along with the much younger Esmee and Guilbert, but he could catch a glimpse of the two girls at the very top step of the stairs. He could see that Azalee was tapping her foot in time to the music. That was Azalee! She was determined not to miss the ball—even though she couldn't be part of the dancing!

Chapter 2

FROM THE TOP OF THE STAIRS AZALEE WATCHED THE dancers. Her face was flushed, and her hair had come loose from the white ribbon that had tied it back in a cascade of neat curls. She loved the sound and rhythm of the music, and she felt as though the beat was echoing in her blood.

Azalee felt exhilarated by the sight of silks and satins and jewels waltzing below her and by the mixture of laughter and music drifting up the stairs to her. She noticed that most of the younger men were in uniform and they looked wonderful. Azalee had heard her father say that the regiment would probably never go into battle, but it was good to know that the young men were prepared to, if it became necessary. They were so handsome—all her friends in the New Orleans Regiment—and so brave. She was proud of them all.

"Look," Marguerite said, "isn't that Alain?"

"Where? I don't see him."

"He just whirled by. With Felice. I think it was Felice. Yes, there he is. Do you see him, Azie? He's dancing with Felice Duchamps."

"I don't care who he's dancing with," Azalee said angrily, as she moved down another step. "Felice! She's eighteen and she still can't dance. I hope she steps all over Alain's feet!"

"Azie," Marguerite whispered, "you'd better come back up here. Someone's sure to see you."

"Let them," she said, and she moved down two more steps.

Let Madame Duval see her, and her father, and Nani Charlotte—and, most important, let Alain see her. She thought he'd come upstairs after he danced one dance with his mother, and now, there he was, dancing with that horrible Felice. Well, she didn't care. Next year, when she could go to all the balls held in New Orleans, she would make sure that she never—absolutely *never*—danced with him! And she moved down two more steps, deaf to Marguerite's "Azie!"

Suddenly, Azalee saw the dancers stop in mid-whirl. The music came to a ragged halt. There was a violin screech, and she heard people shouting. But she couldn't hear what they were saying. Azalee hurried down until she was standing on the second step from the bottom.

Marguerite had followed her, and she was just one step above Azalee. "What's happening?" she asked. "Why has the music stopped?"

"Ssh," Azalee said. "Listen."

"You may not come in here, sir." Azalee recognized Theodore Duval's voice. "You have no right to enter my home."

Azalee couldn't hear the other man's reply, but a

minute later she saw him—a man in an elegant magenta jacket, lace at his cuffs, and a foam of lace at his throat.

"Lafitte!" Azalee heard someone say. "It's Jean Lafitte . . . the pirate . . . Lafitte."

"Azie," Marguerite's voice trembled, "is that *really* Jean Lafitte? The pirate? Let's run upstairs . . . quickly."

"And miss all the excitement? Nothing's going to happen, Marguerite. Not with the New Orleans Regiment right there in the ballroom. They can take care of Monsieur Lafitte."

"But, Azie, he isn't alone."

The girls watched as a strange group of men crowded into the ballroom. Some where dressed in striped jerseys, while others wore elegant jackets in imitation of their captain. It was Jean Lafitte's crew, and they had come into the ballroom armed with sabers and pistols worn casually in their belts.

"You cannot come in here, sir." Theodore Duval was speaking to a man dressed in a uniform. It wasn't the bright-red-jacketed uniform of the New Orleans Regiment. This was the sober blue of the American Army, a uniform rarely seen in New Orleans. New Orleans had only become part of the United States two short years before, and Azalee had heard her father say that he still had trouble thinking of himself as an American.

The man in the blue uniform had his back turned toward her, so Azalee couldn't see him; but she could see Monsieur Duval, who was trying to control his anger. "How dare you enter my home?" he was saying. "Is this what it means to become part of the United States—that any bunch of cutthroats can march into a man's home? Get out!"

"I'm sorry, sir," Azalee heard the man in blue say. "I must talk to you. Your safety and the safety of New Orleans depends upon it."

"*Our* safety?" Azalee recognized her father's voice. "You dare talk about our safety, when you bring Lafitte right into our midst? He's been raiding our ships! We are afraid to leave port with Lafitte skulking outside the harbor, ready to board and sink our merchant fleet—"

"I do not skulk, Monsieur!" Lafitte roared, drowning out everyone else's voice. "I sail openly on the open seas, and, if your men are such poor sailors that they cannot get out of my way, that is their problem—and yours!"

"Sir." Azalee recognized the voice of the man in blue. "Captain Lafitte brings news about the British—news that could save your ships and maybe your lives. If we could talk . . ."

Monsieur Duval suddenly seemed to remember that his ballroom was filled with guests. "Come," he said to the man in blue and to Lafitte. "Come with me. Pierre, please accompany me. Alain, Gerard, Captain Corday—if you will come, too, please."

As Azalee watched, she saw her father and the others follow Theodore Duval into the library. The musicians began to play, but they were so distracted they played unevenly. Besides, no one wanted to dance. Lafitte's crew was bunched up at one side of the ballroom, the guests at the other side. An empty dance floor separated the two groups.

"Look at them," Azalee said to Marguerite. "They may as well form two lines and dance a gavotte!"

"Azie, aren't you frightened?"

"Maybe. Just a little. But it's still better than being upstairs in the nursery."

As the girls watched, Theodore Duval and the others came out of the library. Azalee and Marguerite heard Monsieur Duval explain to his guests that the man in blue was Lieutenant John Trent, an officer in the American Army and an aide to General Andrew Jackson.

After that, the lieutenant explained that Jean Lafitte had joined the Americans against the British and that he was prepared to protect the New Orleans Merchant Fleet against the British Navy.

"Protection? Lafitte will protect us?" A small man with a red handlebar mustache was talking. "That is like asking the fox to protect the chicken coop . . ."

Another man, who Azalee recognized as Monsieur Blanchard, a chief exporter, piped up from the midst of the crowd. "Is that our choice? To be captured by the British or protected by a pirate?"

"Pirate?" Lieutenant Trent addressed Monsieur Blanchard, and Azalee could hear the humor in his voice. "There are no pirates here, gentlemen. This is Captain Lafitte—aide to General Jackson, American patriot, a brave man who is willing to risk his ships to save yours."

"And what is Captain Lafitte getting for his services?"

"I will answer that question myself," Jean Lafitte said. "The general has been good enough to grant me amnesty in return for fighting the British. After the war is over, I will settle down and be another New Orleans shipowner—like the rest of you gentlemen."

Azalee shivered when she heard Lafitte speak. His voice reminded her of a dagger sheathed in velvet—it was smooth and deep, but she could sense the danger beneath the velvet. His voice was in contrast to John Trent's. *He sounds young,* Azalee thought, *younger than that pirate. I wonder what he looks like.*

He may be young, but everyone is listening to him. And they seem to agree with him. Monsieur Duval and Papa, and the others, too—they will go along with him. Azalee knew her father and the other gentlemen were not easy to persuade. She was more and more curious about the young lieutenant who seemed to have New Orleans's top businessmen eating out of the palm of his hand. *I wonder, what does he look like?*

Azalee kicked off her shoes and stood on her stockinged toes, trying to see the man in blue. After what seemed a long while, she heard Monsieur Duval offer everyone a glass of champagne, and finally—finally—the man in blue turned around.

Azalee's heart did flip-flops. He was so good-looking, she could hardly believe it. Alain was handsome, but Alain always looked so orderly, so well put together. This man looked as though he'd be a lot more comfortable in an open shirt than in the high-buttoned jacket of his army uniform. And the way he moved! He looked like a hunter stalking wild game. She had never seen anyone move through a civilized New Orleans home like that. And he was tall, taller even than Alain, who was six feet tall. Staring at him, Azalee tried to guess his age. He looked about twenty.

Azalee's fingers clenched and unclenched. She wanted to run her fingers through that thick mat of streaky light brown hair, and she longed to push that lock of hair off his forehead.

She could see him quite clearly now, because, instead of following the others to the buffet for a glass of champagne, he was staring straight at her and Marguerite. Then he smiled and started coming toward them. No, she was wrong. He wasn't coming toward her and Marguerite—he was coming toward *her*.

Look at her, Johnny Trent thought, as he saw the dark-haired girl standing on the staircase. *Would you just look at her! Pretty as an angel on top of the Christmas tree, except that I bet she's no angel.*

"A glass of champagne?" he heard Theodore Duval ask him, but it wasn't champagne he was interested in.

He walked across the room, drawn like a magnet to the green-eyed girl. He'd heard some of his fellow squirrel shooters from Tennessee talk about the girls of New Orleans, but he hadn't paid much attention. A girl was a girl, and all the girls he had known back home were pretty much alike. Good, hard-working farm girls, girls who could plow and till all day beside a man and then cook him dinner at night.

But this girl! He bet she'd never done a day's work

in her life; bet her hands were soft and white—as white as that fancy dress she had on. But she was more than a pretty, rich girl from New Orleans. There were plenty of them in the ballroom he had just walked through. He could see that. This one was different. Hell, she had kicked off her shoes, and her hair was all loose around her shoulders. There was a wildness about this girl—a wildness that told him she was his kind of girl.

Chapter 3

"AZIE," MARGUERITE'S VOICE WAS TREMBLING, "let's run upstairs—quick."

"You go ahead if you want to," Azalee said, as she stared at the approaching young man. "I'm staying here."

Suddenly, the lieutenant was standing in front of her. "Ma'am, I'm Lieutenant Johnny Trent."

His voice. His voice made her shiver. His drawl was thick—thick as syrup and just as sweet. "Yes," Azalee said, "I know . . . I heard."

Johnny Trent looked only at Azalee. He didn't seem to notice Marguerite standing close by. When she looked into his eyes, Azalee saw they were smoky topaz—the eyes of a cat. But not a tame house cat, she thought. These were the eyes of a wild cat, an animal that might roam the bayous. And the way he looked at her! She had to stop herself from pulling at the shoulders of her gown to make sure that she was completely dressed.

"All that talk," Johnny Trent said in that honey-sweet drawl, "and they never said one interesting thing. Talkin' about New Orleans ships, how come they didn't brag on the New Orleans girls? Now that's something to brag on, seems to me."

Azalee felt as though her cheeks were burning. She always had a smart answer when she flirted with Alain or any of the other young men she knew in New Orleans, but now she couldn't think of a thing to say.

"What's your name?" Johnny Trent asked Azalee. "You going to tell me?"

"It's Azalee. Azalee La Fontaine."

"Well, Miss Azalee, sounds like the music has started up again, so how about a dance?"

Azalee yearned to dance with him. She had never wanted to do anything so much in her whole life, but she just couldn't. She'd disgrace her father, and her grandmother would never forgive her. But if it hadn't been for them, she would have been in this stranger's arms in a second.

"I can't," she said, and her voice was almost a wail.

Johnny Trent's face clouded. Now his eyes were those of a dangerous cat. "Why is that? Not allowed to dance with anyone who isn't in that fancy New Orleans Regiment, is that it?"

"That isn't it," Marguerite said. "We're not allowed to dance with *anyone*—not until we're seventeen."

Azalee was furious! Leave it to Marguerite. What was the point of telling the most handsome man that she had ever seen that she was still being treated like a child?

Johnny Trent looked appraisingly at Azalee. "How old are you? Sixteen?"

Azalee nodded, too ashamed to speak.

"Well, where I come from, sixteen is old enough for lots of things—marriage, sometimes, and dancing for sure," he said, holding his hand out to her. "Miss Azalee—"

"Yes," Azalee said, feeling like she was in a trance. "Just wait until I put my shoes on."

Johnny Trent's mouth turned up in a slow, lazy grin. "With or without shoes, don't matter none to me."

"Azalee," Marguerite wailed, "you *can't!*"

"Sure she can," he said, and Azalee felt two strong hands around her waist. He lifted her off the step and swung her into the air and onto the floor. They took three turns, and they were in the middle of the ballroom.

As he spun her about in a waltz, Azalee glimpsed at her father and grandmother's horrified faces at the edge of the ballroom. She was doing something wrong, something terrible, and they would scold and preach at her for a month, she knew that. But she also knew that she would never give up this sweet feeling, no matter what anyone said to her.

Her head was against Johnny Trent's chest, and she willingly let him pull her closer to him. Her heart pounded and her blood sang, and all she wanted to do was to go on dancing with him forever. *Don't let the music stop,* she prayed silently, *don't let the music ever stop.*

She sure is something, Johnny Trent said to himself. *With a girl like this, a man would never need to look farther.* He couldn't believe that she was actually dancing with him, actually in his arms. The moment he saw her standing on that staircase—her shoes off and her hair kind of wild—he knew that she was the girl for him. She was like a girl from one of his fancier dreams, but she was better than a dream—she was real flesh and blood.

He pulled her closer to him, and his heart pounded as her body curved willingly to his. He heard and felt her sharp intake of breath. She was only sixteen, but Johnny Trent knew that he held a woman in his arms.

The music ended, but they held onto each other, neither wanting the moment to end. The ballroom floor was empty, except for Azalee and Johnny Trent standing in the center of the floor.

He was the first to speak. "Don't tell me the ball is over?"

"The music has stopped," Azalee whispered.

"Not for us," he said, his voice husky. "I still hear the music, don't you?"

"Perhaps we could persuade the musicians to play one more waltz," Azalee heard a voice behind her say, "but the next dance is mine, Lieutenant Trent."

Azalee stepped reluctantly from the circle of Johnny Trent's arms and turned to face the pirate captain, Jean Lafitte.

"I reckon dancing time is over," Johnny said. "We better be getting back to your ship, Captain Lafitte."

"Not without one dance," Jean Lafitte said.

Azalee heard the steel beneath that velvet voice once again. *This man is dangerous*, she thought, *and it could be dangerous for Johnny Trent to cross him.* "Of course," she chattered nervously, "one dance. I'm sure the musicians will play for you again, Captain Lafitte."

Azalee moved woodenly into Jean Lafitte's arms, and the music began. She moved like a puppet on a string, manipulated by the pirate, whose strong arms held her without a touch of tenderness.

As they circled about, Azalee glanced at Johnny Trent's face—dark with anger. *But doesn't he understand? I'm doing this for him.* She looked up at the pirate captain. He was as old as her father, but there was nothing fatherly about him. And while her father's hair was almost all gray, Lafitte had only one white streak running through his dark brown hair. His eyes were steel gray—eyes the color of a dangerously sharpened sword.

Well, just look at her, thought Johnny Trent, suddenly wishing that he wasn't in this fancy house, wearing his fancy uniform, not able to do what he really wanted to do, which was to pull Azalee out of Jean Lafitte's arms. *One minute she's dancing with me, all sweet and loving, and now she's giving the same treatment to Lafitte. No wonder they don't let the girls of New Orleans go dancing before they're seventeen—they're too dangerous. Little Miss Azalee is nothing more than a heartless flirt. Stick to the girls from Tennessee, Johnny Trent. At least a man knows where he is with the likes of them.*

Azalee was relieved when she saw her father speak to the musicians, and the waltz finally ended. Captain Lafitte let go of her reluctantly, and Pierre La Fontaine, followed by Alain Duval, came quickly to his daughter's side. "Azalee," he said, and she heard the warning in her father's voice.

"I—I was just dancing, Papa."

"So I see. And with Captain Lafitte, at that. You've had enough dancing for one night, Azalee—far more than you were supposed to have. It's time we were going home."

"Yes, Papa."

Pierre La Fontaine had his arm protectively about Azalee, but Jean Lafitte stopped them. "Monsieur La Fontaine," he said, "I would be pleased if one day you and your daughter would honor me with a visit. My house is on Grand Terre Island, and I have many art objects that might be of interest to you both."

A visit to the pirate's home! Azalee could see that her father was about to sputter a refusal—a refusal so insulting that it might cause Jean Lafitte to challenge her father to a duel.

"Please, Papa," Azalee tugged at her father's sleeve, "I am tired. I would like to go home."

Just then, Johnny Trent walked over to them. "A lot of dancing for one night," Johnny said, suddenly allied with Azalee's father. "That's enough to make anyone tired."

"There was supposed to be no dancing for Azalee tonight," Alain Duval told John Trent. "Our girls are perhaps not quite as forward as the girls of Tennessee."

Forward! Johnny Trent thought of the mild-mannered girls he had left back home. Maybe they weren't as pretty as this Azalee La Fontaine and they didn't have clothes so fancy, but they sure were a whole lot sweeter. "I wouldn't say that our girls are forward," Johnny said, and there was something dangerous about his drawl. "Let's just say that they know how to take care of themselves—just like the men from Tennessee."

"But that's part of Mademoiselle's charm," Jean Lafitte interrupted, "that she is so used to being taken care of by a man—Papa, of course," and he made a slight bow to Pierre La Fontaine.

Azalee's heart was pounding. Johnny Trent, Alain, her father—all so angry. She felt badly about her father and sorry about Alain, but the one she really cared about was Johnny. She looked at him imploringly. Couldn't he understand that she had only danced with Lafitte to spare him? Had he felt nothing when he held her in his arms?

She wanted to go home—desperately, she wanted to be in her own room. She wanted to solve the puzzle that was Johnny Trent, but once again Jean Lafitte stopped them. "You haven't replied to my invitation, Monsieur."

"Thank you, Captain Lafitte." Azalee spoke before her father could say something insulting to the pirate captain. "My father and grandmother and I would be pleased to visit your home—one day."

Jean Lafitte smiled. He took Azalee's hand, bowed, and kissed it. "French dancing masters and French manners. You have a jewel, Monsieur La Fontaine.

Guard it well. This jewel is worth more than all the ships in New Orleans."

"I need no advice on how to take care of my daughter, sir!" And with his arm about Azalee, Pierre La Fontaine swept past the pirate captain and John Trent.

Johnny. Azalee's appeal could only be a silent one. *Johnny, when will I see you again?* She didn't dare look back at him, afraid the anger in his face would break her heart like a stone thrown against a looking glass.

The next morning, Azalee sat silently at the breakfast table, as Nani Charlotte and her father took turns scolding her. She had looked like a hoyden . . . Her hair had come undone . . . She had actually danced with the two most unsuitable men at the ball . . . Why hadn't she stayed upstairs where she belonged?

Azalee pushed her coffee cup away. She couldn't swallow a mouthful of food. *He's going to come calling. He's got to. The way he made me feel last night, he must have felt the way I did. He just must have!*

Her heart began to pound when Fanchon entered the morning room with the largest bunch of white, pink, and red peonies that Azalee had ever seen. "A man rode up with these," Fanchon said. "He said they are for Mademoiselle Azalee."

"But who are they from?" Pierre La Fontaine asked.

Azalee reached for the flowers before either her grandmother or her father could take them. *They had to be from Johnny.* She searched desperately for a note, pulling the paper away quickly from the long stems, until finally her fingers touched an envelope. But it wasn't just an envelope; there was a small box as well.

"Ivory," Nani Charlotte said with satisfaction. "It must be from Alain Duval. One of the boxes his grandfather brought back when he was trading in China. Open it, Azie."

Azalee was glad that Nani hadn't asked to see the note. Johnny's words would be meant only for her. She opened the box and, nestling in its blue velvet heart, was a tiny, exquisitely carved ivory rose. The flower held a drop of dew, except that this dew drop was a diamond, as perfectly carved as the rose itself.

Azalee's fingers crumpled the note she held hidden in her lap. This couldn't be from Johnny Trent. Such an elaborate, expensive gift. She pushed the peonies away with distaste. Johnny would have been more likely to send her a bouquet of forget-me-nots, or a bunch of she-loves-me, she-loves-me-not daisies.

Nani Charlotte looked smug. She had been afraid that Azalee's behavior last night would so antagonize Alain that he would lose interest in her granddaughter, but that beautiful gift indicated that he still cared for her.

"Isn't there a note, Azie?" her father asked.

"Yes," she answered woodenly, no longer caring if they read the note before she did, "here it is."

Nani Charlotte plucked the note from Azalee's fingers and shrieked when she read it. "Pierre," she said, "Pierre—"

Pierre La Fontaine read the note and began sputtering. "How dare he! How dare he! I should have challenged him to a duel last night when he had the audacity to ask Azalee to dance with him."

Azalee took the note from her father and read it out loud. "A flower of ivory for a girl who is more beautiful than any flower." The note was signed with a scrawled signature, but there was no mistaking the large *J* and the looped *L*—Jean Lafitte. He had sent her the flowers and the jewel.

"I will send that—that bauble back to the thief at once!" Pierre La Fontaine said. "That stolen jewel. Who knows what poor dead woman once owned it!"

Azalee shivered and pushed the ivory box and the ivory flower away. Her ivory rose had been dipped in blood.

Jean Lafitte had obviously misunderstood her willingness to dance with him, and she was beginning to realize that Johnny Trent had misunderstood it, as well. But how could he have? Azalee remembered the sweet feeling she had known when she had danced with the tall man in blue from Tennessee. If only she could see him once again—if only they could have a chance to be together.

She looked at her father and her grandmother and decided that they were right about her. She was too careless, too reckless—and now her reckless behavior had cost her the only man she would ever care for.

29

"I'm sorry, Papa," she said, close to tears. "Nani Charlotte, I'll try to behave better from now on. I promise. You'll see." And all the time she was thinking, *Johnny, give me another chance, please—give me another chance*.

Chapter 4

"Azie," Nani Charlotte said, two days later, "you've been moping in the house for days. Are you feeling well?"

"I'm fine, Nani," Azalee said, but she couldn't tell anyone that she didn't feel fine at all.

Not one word, not one note, not a request to visit her—nothing had come from Johnny Trent. Forget him, she told herself every morning when a new day started; forget him, she said every night before she went to bed. But it was no use. She thought of him all day, and he haunted her dreams all night.

Nani Charlotte looked shrewdly at her. She knew something was wrong with her granddaughter, but she didn't know what it was. "Fanchon is going to the market today," she said. "Pehaps you would like to go with her."

Azalee shrugged. Usually, she loved the open-air markets, loved walking among the stalls, drinking the hot black coffee that always seemed better than the coffee at home. But now she just hated to leave the house. What if she missed a note or a visit from Johnny Trent? But she noticed her grandmother's stare and decided that it would be easier to go along with Nani Charlotte.

"I'll go," Azalee said, "and maybe Marguerite will come with me."

"That's fine," Nani Charlotte said. "I like Marguerite. Such a well-brought-up young lady."

Azalee sighed. Nani said nothing more. She decided not to continue lecturing her granddaughter; the child had looked a little pensive the last two days.

Azalee sat in the carriage beside Fanchon. They arrived at the open-air market and waited for a few minutes, until the Brevard carriage with Marguerite and Phillipine, the housekeeper, pulled up beside theirs. "Marguerite," Azalee called out, "Marguerite—"

"Quietly," Fanchon said. "It is not necessary to shout, Azie."

"Oh, Fanchon, not you, too. Everyone is always telling me to walk more slowly, speak more quietly. Some days I think no one wants me to feel alive!"

"Go ahead, Azie," Fanchon relented. "Go with Marguerite. But don't go too far. Phillipine and I will be right with you."

"Yes, I know," Azalee said. "No nice girl is ever seen in public without a chaperone—at least, not until she's married."

"Yes," Fanchon said, "because, when she's married, she has her husband beside her as an escort."

"As a chaperone, you mean," Azie said. "I don't think there's much of a difference."

"You'll see the difference when you get married," Fanchon said. "Time enough to talk about it then."

"What's the use of getting married, if you can never go anywhere alone?" Azalee asked. "Boys and men have all the fun."

"Sometimes I wish you were more like your mother," Fanchon said. "She never would have talked that way!" The Haitian woman sighed. "Well, go ahead—go talk to Marguerite. Phillipine and I will meet you at Monsieur Louis's coffee stand."

The two girls had much to talk about, since they hadn't seen each other since the night of the Duval hall.

"You danced with Jean Lafitte and with that handsome lieutenant! What was it like, Azie?"

For a moment, Azalee tried to be nonchalant, tried to pretend that the evening had been nothing special. But she couldn't pretend to Marguerite. "It was wonderful," she said, and, when she thought of Johnny Trent, her heart began to pound. "It was the best night of my life."

"Have you heard from him?" Marguerite asked.

"Who?"

"That lieutenant," Marguerite said. "Who else would I mean? Certainly not that pirate."

Azalee couldn't bear to reveal to Marguerite that there was no word from Johnny Trent. She didn't want her friend to know how she really felt. What had happened to the carefree Azalee La Fontaine? She didn't want anyone to know how much that one dance with Johnny had affected her, and she decided to be as frivolous as always.

"But, Marguerite," she said, "that's exactly who I did hear from—the pirate, Captain Lafitte."

"Azie—no!"

"Yes! And he sent me flowers and a jewel."

"But, why? What does it mean?"

Azalee stopped beside a woman who was selling candies from a large covered basket. She reached into her small embroidered purse and took out a few coins to buy pralines for herself and Marguerite. This was an important conversation, and important conversations always made her hungry.

"I don't know what it means," Azalee chattered. "Imagine—meeting Jean Lafitte! And on a night when I wasn't even supposed to be dancing." But it wasn't Lafitte she remembered, it was Johnny.

Marguerite looked properly shocked. Good! That was what Azalee wanted. There was no need for anyone to know how she really felt about Johnny Trent.

She felt better. The best thing to do about a broken heart, she realized, was to hide it. She had to do something—anything—to help her forget Johnny. That was when she got the idea about riding out to the bayou country to see Madame Pompom.

"Marguerite," she said, "everything is so dull right now in New Orleans. All this boring talk about the war. Let's ride out tomorrow to see Madame Pompom. She could read our palms and tell us about the future."

Marguerite needed to be persuaded. What if they were captured by the British? Or the pirates? Or any of the other dangerous men roaming the bayous?

"The pirates are on our side now," Azalee said. "You heard that. And we'll ask Gerard and Alain to ride with us. They're coming for coffee this afternoon. They'd be a match for a whole army of British."

"Would they come with us?" Marguerite asked.

"If I ask Alain, he'll come," Azalee said. "He'll be glad that I forgave him for dancing with that old Felice."

That afternoon Azalee was on her best behavior, when Madame Duval, accompanied by her two sons, came to visit.

Her grandmother poured coffee into the delicate white porcelain cups, and Azalee handed it around. "A biscuit?" she asked Madame Duval. "Sugar, Madame?"

Madame Duval looked up at Azalee, suddenly the sweet, demure young girl. The girl was doing her best to make up for her terrible behavior at the ball, Madame Duval thought. She looked from Azalee to her two sons, so handsome in their uniforms. But they were at war with the British, and so, those uniforms frightened her. How many more days of peace would they have? How many more days would they be able to flirt with a pretty girl? "Yes," she said abruptly.

"One biscuit, Azalee, and no sugar. You know I never take sugar. Why don't you young people go into the music room, or to the garden? I would like to talk to Madame La Fontaine alone."

Azalee, Alain, and Gerard were happy to go off to the garden, and, as they strolled beside Pierre La Fontaine's much-prized rosebushes, Azalee told them that she and Marguerite wanted to ride with them into bayou country the next day.

"We'd have to get permission from Captain Corday," Gerard said.

"And he'd never give it," Alain added. "We're not permitted to ride that far from the city. The British attack could come at any time."

"Then Marguerite and I will just have to go without you," Azalee said.

"You can't do that, Azie," Alain protested. "You won't be safe."

"We'll have to manage," Azalee insisted. "I want to see Madame Pompom. Of course, if Felice Duchamps asked you to ride with her, you'd never say no . . ."

"That's not true," Alain protested.

"Isn't it? You spent all evening dancing with her at the ball."

"I had to dance with someone," Alain said angrily. "You were so busy with that provincial soldier, and with that pirate—"

"Provincial?" Azalee said. "Perhaps Johnny Trent is provincial, but he's a marvelous dancer . . . and so is Captain Lafitte," she quickly added, not wanting Alain to spot her real feelings about Johnny Trent.

"That pirate!"

"He's more than a pirate now, much more. Who knows? One day he may be the most important man in New Orleans . . . and I may be his wife," she said teasingly.

"Wife to a pirate?"

Alain was ready to believe anything that she told him. Well, better that he thought she was interested in Jean Lafitte than to know who she really yearned for. "He won't be a pirate by then," Azalee told him. "That's why I want to see Madame Pompom tomorrow. She knows what will happen in the future."

"That old witch," Alain protested, "knows nothing."

"You're wrong," Azalee insisted. "Of course, she's a witch; that much is true. But it's witches who know things like that."

"I won't let you and Marguerite ride into bayou country by yourselves. I'll tell your father."

Azalee whirled and faced him. "Do that, Alain, and I will never—*never*—talk to you again."

Alain tried to laugh. "You've said that before, Azie. You know you don't mean it."

"I mean it this time."

Gerard looked at Azalee and his brother. He knew how much his brother loved her, knew that Alain would be miserable if he lost her. "Alain," he said softly, "we must ride with Azie and Marguerite tomorrow."

His brother's words helped Alain back out of a difficult situation. He didn't want to give in to Azalee, but he didn't want to lose her either. He could pretend now that he was going because his brother had insisted. "All right, Gerard, we'll go—if you think it's a good idea."

Azalee shrugged. She didn't care why Alain had changed his mind, just as long as he and Gerard agreed to go with them. It was the only way her father and Nani Charlotte would agree to let her go riding at all.

"And Marguerite is going, too?" Nani Charlotte asked for what seemed like the hundredth time.

"Yes, Nani, I told you so."

"And Alain and Gerard?"

"Yes, yes, Alain and Gerard, too—absolutely."

"You mustn't ride too far from the city or regiment headquarters," her father said.

"No, Papa—not too far."

"Besides, Gerard and Alain would be in a great deal of trouble if they rode far from the city. They're under orders, and they have to be ready to report to the regiment at a moment's notice."

How boring it all was, Azalee thought. Everyone unable to take care of themselves. That was another reason why she was so eager to see Madame Pompom. Maybe she could tell her when she would be married and able to lead her own life. The most important reason was, of course, that Madame Pompom might be able to reveal the very name of the man she'd marry.

Madame Johnny Trent. The name went through her mind. It wasn't a familiar name in New Orleans, but she liked it. *Why hasn't he called on me?* she thought for the hundredth time.

Chapter 5

═══════ ❦ ═══════

WHEN ALAIN AND GERARD ARRIVED AT THE LA FONtaine house early the next afternoon, they were surprised to see that Azalee's favorite mare, Cinderella, was wearing a sidesaddle.

Alain looked at Azalee in her dove gray sidesaddle habit, complete with long skirt and a veiled hat perched over one eyebrow. "You are riding sidesaddle?" he asked. "I thought that you would have borrowed a pair of your father's riding breeches."

Azalee slowly raised her emerald-green eyes to him. "Breeches? Me? Alain, I wouldn't go so improperly dressed."

Alain shook his head. She surprised him sometimes. He cupped his hand to hold one booted foot, and, as he helped her mount, he could see that beneath her skirt she wore breeches. He smiled. She was still Azalee— the most spirited girl in New Orleans.

Azalee knew that he had seen the breeches beneath the skirt, and she was glad that he had smiled and not scolded. In thanks, her small, gloved hand held onto his a moment longer than necessary.

Azalee, Alain, and Gerard rode off to the Brevard house. Alain watched while his brother helped Marguerite mount. He was sure that Marguerite would never dream of wearing her father's riding breeches beneath her long habit. Marguerite always did the right thing, always said the right thing. She was warm and kind and easy to be with.

He had known both girls ever since they were all children. He had never had a disagreement with Marguerite, while with Azalee he had had many arguments. But it was Azalee who made his heart pound, it was Azalee who made his head swim—not Marguerite.

Alain thought of John Trent and Jean Laffite, and he was angry once again. His Azalee in another man's arms. She didn't know it, but that's how he thought of her—*his Azalee.* He looked at her riding beside him. She rode easily and expertly, and her hands held the reins with confidence. Every now and then she would lean forward to pat the mare's neck, and the animal responded by adding an extra high step to her canter.

The four rode decorously, as long as they were close to New Orleans, close to where others could see them. Soon they left the city and were riding on a road where the houses were at a greater distance from each other. They were on the outskirts of New Orleans, and, in a little while, there would be houses at all.

Azalee spurred her horse to a gallop, and Alain clicked to his mount, so that he could catch up with her. "Not so fast, Azie," he said. "These narrow paths—they're dangerous."

"Not for me," Azalee said, and she leaned over her mare, urging her forward.

Azalee rode on ahead, with Alain behind her and the other two far behind. It was only when the path wove its way around the dark canals of still water that Azalee slowed her horse to a trot. She had never ridden this far into the bayou country before. She hadn't known that it was so dark—so silent. "Alain," she said, as he caught up with her, "are you sure that this is the right road? It seems so ghostly."

"There are ghosts here. Ghosts of the first French who settled here and the ghost of Captain Jacques Normand—his ghost roams the bayous."

"Who's Jacques Normand?" she asked.

"Another pirate," Alain said, "like your friend Lafitte. Only he was killed by Indians—no one had to hang him, which is probably what will happen to Lafitte."

"Alain, you're not being fair."

Alain reined his horse in and put his hand over Azalee's. His dark brown eyes looked warmly at her. Her mare snorted and came to a halt. Alain turned in his saddle. Gerard and Marguerite were behind them, and still hadn't turned the last bend in the road.

"It wasn't fair of you, Azie, to dance with that man Trent and with Lafitte. I had always thought that, when you appeared at your very first ball, your first dance would be mine."

Alain was hurt, Azalee could see that. But why hadn't he come to sweep her off the steps? Why hadn't he insisted that she dance with him the night of the ball? His mother would never have said a word if Alain had demanded that she be his partner. She thought of Johnny Trent and pulled her hand away from Alain. It would be so much simpler if she could feel about Alain the way she felt about Johnny. But she couldn't dictate those feelings to her rebellious heart.

"You should have claimed that first dance," she said. "I was waiting, sitting there on that staircase . . . but you didn't come."

"You weren't supposed to be dancing that night, Azie. You were supposed to be upstairs—"

"Supposed to do this, supposed to do that," she said impatiently. "You're always worried about what I'm supposed to do!" Azalee signaled her horse, and Cinderella moved into a gallop.

Alain didn't catch up with her until the third bend in the road. He nearly rode past her, because she had dismounted and was standing beside Cinderella, and both were almost obscured by a large weeping willow tree.

"Looking for me?" she called out.

"Azie, what's the matter? Why did you dismount?"

He reined his horse in and looked at her. She had slipped out of her voluminous skirt and was standing beside Cinderella in breeches, boots, and shirt. She smiled up at him. "Isn't this better?"

Alain wanted to tell her that she looked wonderful, and was wonderful—his Azalee, so free, natural, and unafraid. But instead, he said, "I don't know if it's better or not. I just know it's lucky there isn't anyone here to see you. And what are you going to do with all the clothes you've taken off? You'll still have to carry them, even though you're not wearing them."

"No, I won't. Look," she said, pointing to the neat pile she had made beneath the willow tree. There was her skirt and jacket, with the veiled hat on top. "There's no one here to steal them, and who would want them, anyway? Silly clothes. This is the way I like to ride."

Alain started to dismount, so that he could help her climb into the saddle. "Don't bother," she said, and, before he had gotten out of his saddle, she had already put one foot in the stirrup and climbed into hers.

"Clothes or no clothes," Alain said, "you still have to use the saddle the way it was meant to be used—as a sidesaddle."

"I don't care," Azalee replied. "It's still more comfortable without that long skirt and tight jacket. Not to mention that silly hat."

You looked adorable in that silly hat, Alain thought. "Now you look like a boy," he told her.

"I don't care what I look like," Azalee said. "I just want to get to Madame Pompom's. Are we near?"

"Just a few minutes more," Alain said. "Why are you so interested in seeing her? What can she tell you?"

"She can tell me if there's a pirate in my future," Azalee retorted. "A pirate who won't mind if I do look like a boy some of the time. A pirate who thinks I'm a jewel no matter what I'm wearing." *Or a lieutenant from Tennessee,* she thought, *who will love me even if I'm not the perfect lady.* But she didn't want to talk to

Alain about Johnny Trent. She didn't want him or anyone else to know how she felt about the man in blue.

"You're right," Alain answered, "a pirate wouldn't care what you were wearing—a pirate wouldn't know any better. Maybe you do belong with pirates—"

"Azie, you look wonderful," Gerard said, as he and Marguerite caught up with them.

Azalee looked at Alain's brother. "Thank you, Gerard. You mean you don't think I look like a boy?"

Gerard laughed. *"Nothing* could make you look like a boy," he told her.

"But what about your clothes?" Marguerite asked. "Your riding habit? You're not going to go home dressed like this?"

"I'll pick up my clothes on the way back," Azalee said. "We're taking the same road back, aren't we, Alain?"

"We have to—it's the only road. Look to the right. You see that clearing? The cabin? That's where Madame Pompom lives."

"At last," Azalee said. She spurred Cinderella and was the first one to arrive at the clearing and the first one off her horse.

Madame Pompom's house was a cabin built of split logs. It looked deserted. No smoke came from the chimney, and no light shone from within.

"She's not here," Azalee called to the others. "We've come all this way for nothing—"

"Perhaps that depends on what you've come for, *m'petite,*" a voice said.

Azalee spun around. She hadn't heard the old woman come up behind her, hadn't seen her until she stood there—a tiny woman, her hair hidden in a red kerchief, her bright blue eyes remarkably clear and young looking in her dark, lined face.

"I—I didn't see you," Azalee stammered. "Where did you come from?"

"I didn't come," the old woman said. "I've always been here. You are the one who has come."

"But just a minute ago . . . I didn't even see you—"

"A minute ago you didn't know how to look," the old woman said, "or where."

"Alain," Azalee called out, suddenly afraid. "Alain—"

"Alain," the old woman mimicked, "Alain. A minute ago you didn't want him and now you can't do without him. Isn't that so, *m'petite?*"

"Alain—"

"I'm here, Azie," Alain said as he dismounted. "I thought you said no one was here. But you were wrong, Azie. This is Madame Pompom."

"I know," Azalee said. "I'm often wrong about many things."

Madame Pompom cackled. "Good, good. Admit when you're wrong, *m'petite*. Admit it while you can."

This strange old woman frightened Azalee. She was no Fanchon ready to help her with a few simple spells.

"Madame Pompom," Alain said, "we've come because—"

"I know why you've come, little soldier boy.

45

You've come for the same reason everyone comes—to ask something of Madame Pompom. Everyone asks, everyone takes from Madame Pompom, but nobody gives—nobody cares if Madame Pompom lives or dies."

Alain reached into his saddlebag. "You're wrong, Madame Pompom. We're not like everyone. We brought you something, see?"

Madame Pompom snatched the bottle of rum that Alain held out to her. "You are a good little soldier boy," she said. "For this I will answer your question—but just one question for this," and she waved the bottle of rum.

"I have no questions, Madame Pompom," Alain said.

"No questions? Not even one? Is it because you don't believe in Madame Pompom's answers, little soldier boy?"

Alain shook his head. "I can wait to know what tomorrow will bring. But this lady here," he indicated Azalee, "and that one," he pointed to Marguerite, who was just dismounting, "have questions."

Madame Pompom looked from Azalee to Marguerite. "This one first," she said, pointing to Marguerite, "because she is gentle and because she is afraid. Let her be first."

"No!" Marguerite cried out. "Azie, you go first."

Madame Pompom opened the bottle and took a deep drink of rum. "Don't be afraid, little angel," she said. "Madame Pompom cannot hurt a little angel like you. Come, don't be afraid."

Marguerite held out her hand timidly. Madame Pompom took it and rubbed her thumb over the few lines in Marguerite's palm. "A nice hand," she murmured, "and a nice life. That is what I see for this little angel. One love, one man, one marriage, and three children. That is what I see."

"I could have predicted that," Azalee murmured.

Madame Pompom whirled. "But you," she said to Azalee. "I am sure I will not see such peaceful things in your hand. I am sure that's not what I will find there. No! Quick, give me your hand!"

She obeyed, and Madame Pompom gripped her hand roughly, pulling Azalee toward her. "Just as I thought," she laughed, "just as I thought!"

"What is it?" Azalee asked. "What do you see?"

Madame Pompom looked at her slyly. "I see many things. Are you sure you want to know what it is that I see?"

Azalee's heart was pounding, and she wasn't at all sure that she wanted to know what Madame Pompom saw in her hand. Maybe it would be better not to know.

"Well," Madame Pompom tugged at her hand, "is it yes? Is it no? Shall Madame Pompom speak?"

Azalee heard the screech of an owl, and she jumped. Back in New Orleans it was light and bright and sunny, but, in the bayou swamps, the trees and Spanish moss blotted out the sun.

"Well, *m'petite*," Madame Pompom said softly, "afraid?"

Azalee shook her head. She was afraid, but she would never admit it—not to this old woman, not to Alain, who would make fun of her, not to Gerard or Marguerite, who would be too understanding, her fear mirroring theirs. "No," she said. "No, I'm not afraid. Yes, Madame Pompom. Tell me what you see in my hand."

"Ah," Madame Pompom's thumb traced the lines in Azalee's palm. "The line is broken—you see it here? Broken. There will not be only one man in your life—no, that is not for you . . ."

"That much is true," Alain said bitterly.

"Three," Madame Pompom said. "I see three men. Two will love you and leave you, one will pretend to love, and one will return. Yes, one will return . . ."

"But which one?" Azalee asked. "Which one will return? What does he look like, the one who will return?"

Madame Pompom shrugged. "What does he look like? He looks like a man. What does it matter?"

"But who is he? What does he do? Is he much older than I am—the one who will return?"

Madame Pompom looked at her palm once again. "Yes. When he returns he will be older. Yes. I can see that."

Jean Lafitte. He was the man who was older. Alain and Johnny were young. Azalee felt a pang of disappointment. Madame Pompom was predicting that she would marry Lafitte, and not Johnny Trent. But that was silly, and she was nothing but a silly old woman.

She probably saw nothing in her hand, absolutely nothing. Azalee quickly snatched her hand away.

Alain, too, thought of Jean Lafitte. "This is enough!" he said.

"Right," Gerard said, stepping forward, "give the rest of us a chance, Azie. What do you see in my hand, Madame Pompom?"

Madame Pompom laughed. "For one bottle of rum? You want me to do all this work for just one bottle of rum?"

"Of course not," Gerard said. "Here." He reached into his pocket and brought out three silver coins.

"Will this do, Madame Pompom? For me and my brother?"

"For you alone," Alain said, "I told you—I have no desire to know my future."

Madame Pompom grasped Gerard's hand. She frowned. "I see danger, yes, danger . . . and sadness. But here—this line tells me that all will be well with you. But only after the sadness and the danger have passed."

Gerard smiled. "That's all right," he said. "As long as everything comes out all right in the end, I won't mind the sadness and danger."

Madame Pompom looked at him. "You are very young, very young. And I am very old and very tired." She turned from them. "Go away now—all of you—go away."

"Not yet," Gerard said. "Come on, Madame Pompom, tell my brother what you see in his future."

"No, no," Alain said. "I told you I wasn't interested, Gerard."

"Come on, Alain," Gerard insisted, "we've all done it—it's amusing."

"Amusing!" Madame Pompom spat out the word.

"All right," Alain said, "but after that, we must ride back." He held out his hand to Madame Pompom.

She took his hand and studied it for what seemed like a long time. "Little soldier boy," she crooned, "I see—I see nothing."

"How can that be?" Gerard asked. "How can you see nothing in his hand, when you saw so much in ours? How can that be?"

"Because that is the way it is," Madame Pompom said. "My gift comes and goes. Besides, the little soldier boy does not believe. It is hard to read the hand of one who does not believe."

"I agree," Alain said. "Now let's ride out of here. Azie, all of you, mount up. *Au revoir,* Madame Pompom. Thank you."

"I'm glad you don't believe, little soldier boy," Madame Pompom said softly. "It is better so."

The four friends mounted their horses. As they rode off, Alain turned and looked back. He saluted the old woman, who was standing there looking after him.

"Good-bye, little solider boy," she whispered, and even after he had reached the road, her words echoed after him. *Good-bye, little soldier boy.*

Chapter 6

AZALEE WAS QUIET AS THEY RODE TOWARD NEW Orleans. *Three men.* Madame Pompom had said there would be three men in her life—and there were three already. She didn't like the idea that two would leave and that only one would return. Would Johnny Trent be the one who would leave her? Since she hadn't heard from him, maybe that meant he had left her already.

Or maybe it would be Jean Lafitte who would love and leave, and Johnny who would only pretend to love. As for the man who would love, and leave, and return—well, she didn't need Madame Pompom to tell her who that would be. Clearly, it was Alain; good, faithful, slightly dull Alain. Alain, who was always telling her how to behave, telling her what to do. There! He was doing it again.

"You cannot ride into New Orleans dressed in your father's breeches," he was saying. "Didn't you leave your clothes under that big tree over there?"

"Yes, Alain."

"Good. Put them on."

This time Azalee let Alain dismount first, so that he could help her off Cinderella. She pushed aside the curtain of willow branches, but, when she came back to Alain's side, she was still in her breeches. "Alain—"

"Come on, Azie, time to dress and go home."

"But Alain—"

"Azie, put your riding habit on."

"I can't—my clothes are gone. Look!" She parted the willow branches.

"Are you sure this is the place?" Alain asked. "The right tree?"

"Of course, I'm sure. Who could have taken them, Alain? I thought nobody lived around here, except Madame Pompom."

"I thought so, too," Alain said.

"Nani Charlotte will send me to a convent when she sees me dressed like this," Azalee said. "I just know she will."

It was Marguerite who came up with an idea. "Let's ride home quickly," she said, "and before we get to New Orleans, I can ride ahead. I'll bring back one of my habits for you, Azie. You can say you fell and tore your skirt, and that I had to give you one of mine—"

"Me? Fall off a horse? Who would believe that?"

"This is no time to brag about your horsemanship," Alain exploded. "We will do as Marguerite suggested. It's the only way. Now, let's ride."

The four of them rode as quickly as they could, but the road was narrow and meandering, and they could never let their horses stretch out into a real gallop.

They were close to New Orleans when they heard the sound of horses, a sound that came closer and closer. "The British," Alain whispered to Gerard. "I've heard that they have scouting parties around New Orelans."

"Or Lafitte's men," Gerard said.

"Pirates? They don't know how to ride. No, it's the British. I wish there were another road out of here."

"The only other way out of here is by boat," Gerard said, "and we don't have a boat. Besides, we couldn't leave the horses."

"I'd rather leave the horses than be captured by the British," Alain said.

"Maybe it isn't the British," Gerard suggested. "It could be the American Army."

"There's a patch of dry land up ahead," Alain said. "If we reach it in time, we can stop there. The trees might hide us. Tell Marguerite and I'll talk to Azie. But let's not frighten them."

Gerard spoke to Marguerite, and Alain told Azalee of their plan. "I'm sorry, Alain," Azalee said. "I've probably gotten you and Gerard into trouble, and Marguerite, too. I'm sorry."

"Spilt milk," Alain said. "No need to talk about it now. Let's see if we can get out of this fix."

Azalee smiled at Alain. She didn't appreciate him enough, and it was times like this that she realized it. Now, when he really would have had good reasons to scold her, he was only concerned with getting them back to safety. Now she was certain that Alain was the man Madame Pompom spoke of—the man who would love and leave and return.

They rode for five minutes more, and the sound of horses coming toward them grew louder and louder. Then, before they could find a place to hide, a troop of soldiers rounded a curve in the road.

Azalee spotted the red jackets and called out, "It's all right, Alain, it's the New Orleans Regiment—we're safe."

"I would have preferred the British," Gerard said.

"Or the Americans," Alain commented.

"I don't understand," Azalee said. "We're safe."

"Safe," Alain said, "and in trouble."

A minute later they came face to face with Captain Corday. "Lieutenant Duval," the captain said to Alain, his round red face even redder than usual. "What are you doing here? Were you sent out on patrol?"

"No, sir," Alain said. "My brother and I were escorting the ladies on a ride into the bayous."

"A ride? Into bayou country?" The captain was incensed. "There is a war going on, and you decide to take the young ladies for a ride? What if you had run into a troop of the British?"

Alain didn't answer, and Azalee said, "Please, don't blame Alain, Captain Corday. It was my idea."

Captain Corday ignored her. She didn't exist as far as he was concerned.

"Well, Lieutenant, what do you have to say?"

"Nothing, sir," Alain answered.

"In addition to endangering your lives and the lives

of these young ladies," the captain said to Alain and Gerard, "you both are absent without official leave. You were told not to ride out of the city, because the regiment could be called into battle at any time. What if the British had attacked New Orleans? What then? You gentlemen deserted your posts!"

Alain and Gerard said nothing. Captain Corday turned to his men. "Sergeant, you will escort these young women to their homes. Lieutenant Valery, you will place Alain and Gerard Duval under arrest. Sergeant, give the commands."

It was while they were riding back to New Orleans that Azalee saw her riding habit strapped to the sergeant's pack. She spurred her horse and rode past the troop of men in red uniforms, bringing Cinderella up beside Captain Corday.

"Captain," she said, "one of your men found my riding habit. May I have it back?"

"You may not," Captain Corday said. "Your father and Monsieur Brevard made me turn out the entire regiment to go hunting for you. We left New Orleans completely unprotected to go searching for two young women who wanted to go for a ride! You've been gone most of the day, and your families are frantic. We found your riding clothes, because we were looking for you, and I think it's fitting that you should ride back to New Orleans dressed exactly as you are. Now, you will ride back to the sergeant. I have no further words for you."

Azalee returned to her place at the rear of the

regiment. They had been gone most of the day—of course her father and Nani Charlotte were worried. The bayou country was so dark, she had no idea that they had been away for hours.

Azalee felt as though the entire city of New Orleans had turned out to see them ride in. She had never seen so many people grouped in the streets, nor so many women taking the air on their wrought-iron balconies.

When they reached the Place d'Armes, Alain and Gerard were escorted to regimental headquarters, while Azalee, Marguerite, and the sergeant continued down the street.

Marguerite was close to tears. "Azie," she said, "what can I tell my parents?"

"The truth," Azalee said. "There's nothing else to do, Marguerite. Just tell the truth."

Azalee sat as straight as she could in her sidesaddle, and it was obvious to everyone that she was dressed in breeches.

They arrived at the Brevard home, where a grim Monsieur Brevard was waiting for Marguerite. "Into the house," was all he said to his daughter, without even a glance for Azalee.

Now it was just Azalee and the sergeant who rode the remaining mile to the La Fontaine home. Azalee wanted to gallop, but the sergeant kept their horses at a leisurely walk. She wondered if he was amused at the way people were looking at her and whispering.

They were almost at home when he allowed their horses to trot. "It wasn't my idea," he explained to Azalee. "It was Captain Corday. He ordered me to take the horses at a walk. I'm sorry, Mademoiselle La Fontaine."

"It's all right," Azalee said. "It doesn't matter—nothing matters any more."

They arrived at the La Fontaine home and, unlike at the Brevards', there was no one waiting out front. "Thank you, Sergeant," Azalee said. "May I have my riding clothes now, please?"

"I'm sorry, but Captain Corday ordered me to deliver them—and you—to your father."

Azalee led the way up the walk to the house. Fanchon opened the door, and Azalee and the sergeant went into the salon, where Pierre La Fontaine and Nani Charlotte waited.

The sergeant saluted. "Captain Corday's compliments, sir. He asked me to give you this," he handed the bundle of clothing to Pierre La Fontaine, "and to make sure that Mademoiselle La Fontaine arrived home safely."

"Thank you, Sergeant," Pierre La Fontaine said. "Very kind of you and Captain Corday."

"Yes, sir." The sergeant saluted once again, and, with a pitying glance at Azalee, he left the house.

Azalee was sorry to see him leave. She knew that her father would never say anything to her in front of a stranger.

"Azalee," Pierre La Fontaine began. "Azalee—"

"Please, Papa," Azalee interrupted. "I am sorry, truly I am. I didn't mean to disgrace you. We were just going for a short ride. I never thought we would be gone for so long—"

"Azalee," her grandmother said, "that's just the trouble—you never think. You always do things without thinking."

"Not always—"

"Often! Too often. You're always sorry later, we know that, too. But it is too late; the damage has been done."

"But, Nani," Azalee said. "What damage? Nothing happened, not really."

"Not really?" Pierre La Fontaine said. "Alain and Gerard Duval are in terrible trouble, the four of you could have been captured by British infiltrators, the city could have been attacked—"

"But, Papa, we weren't captured, the city wasn't attacked—"

"In other words, you would do the same thing again? Is that it? And what is your reason for coming home in that disgraceful outfit? Do you have some excuse for that?"

Azalee hung her head. "No, Papa," she said.

"What *are* you wearing? What is that costume you have on?" Pierre La Fontaine came closer. "Why, they're my breeches—my good riding breeches from France."

"But, Papa, you said they no longer fit you. I heard you say that—"

"Azalee, go to your room!"

"Yes, Papa."

Azalee was glad to escape to her room. She wanted to be alone to think. Her father and Nani Charlotte were very angry. What would they do? They would probably not let her go riding for a week, or maybe a month. Maybe they wouldn't let her go to any afternoon parties for a while. She was sure they wouldn't let her see Gerard or Alain, and maybe not even Marguerite.

Her father and Nani Charlotte—she loved them both so much. Yet, she always managed to hurt them. She didn't mean to—she never meant to—but she knew that they were disappointed in her. She looked at her mother's picture and picked it up to examine it more closely. "I wish I could be more like you, Mama, truly I do—but I just can't."

That night at dinner Azalee learned that Alain and Gerard had been released from house arrest and were put on extra guard duty as a punishment. She learned that Marguerite had been scolded and sent to her room without dinner. And she learned just what her father had planned for her.

"If it wasn't for the war," Pierre La Fontaine said, "I'd send you to France. There's a fine finishing school at a convent in the mountains near Chamonix. That would be the perfect place for you, Azalee."

A convent school! That would be terrible, Azalee thought. No parties, no riding; just discipline, lessons, and classes in deportment. She would die locked up in a place like that.

"But, unfortunately," her father continued, "because of the war, I can't send you to France. The trip would be too dangerous." Azalee breathed a sigh of relief. "However, I am sending you to stay with Aunt Paulette."

"But Aunt Paulette lives in a tiny village, Papa. Just a few houses and a church."

"Exactly. A few houses and a church. Nothing that can get you into more trouble."

"But I don't know anyone there, Papa. I won't have any friends."

"I know that," her father said. "You will be in a quiet place, without distractions. Maybe that will cure your recklessness, your thoughtlessness."

"But, Papa, there's nothing to do there."

"I certainly hope not," her grandmother said. "I hope there is not one single afternoon party and not one young man for you to flirt with. We are doing this for your own good, Azalee."

"But, Papa," Azalee was close to tears, "I'll miss you and Nani Charlotte. I'll be so homesick, I'll die . . ."

"Now, Azie—" Pierre La Fontaine looked less sure of himself.

"Pierre," Nani Charlotte said, "don't weaken. It's time you stopped letting Azalee wind you around her little finger."

"I don't do that, Nani."

"Yes, you do, my beautiful Azalee," Nani Charlotte said. "You wind both of us around your little finger. We have let you have your way far too often, Azie," her voice broke. "Don't you see? If anything had happened to you today, Pierre and I would have died. We must teach you to be more careful. We must save you from yourself. It's the only way."

At that, Azalee burst into tears. Her grandmother began to cry, too. "It's the only way, Azie," she said once again. "We are doing this for your own good."

Chapter 7

AZALEE COULDN'T BELIEVE IT. HER FATHER WAS really sending her away. She stood on the dock, her trunks beside her and a silent Fanchon standing nearby.

Her father was on board the *Isabella*, the finest sailing ship of the La Fontaine fleet, the ship that was to take her to her Aunt Paulette.

She had visited her aunt many years before and remembered a large white house surrounded by quiet fields and bayous. That was the word to describe Aunt Paulette's life—*quiet*. Far too quiet for Azalee.

Pierre La Fontaine came down the gangplank. "Your cabin is ready, Azie. You will have to share it with Fanchon."

"But, Papa, what about the British warships? And we don't even have one of Captain Lafitte's ships to escort us."

"The *Isabella* doesn't need to be escorted by pirates. The captain isn't taking her far out."

Azalee turned to her father again. "Papa," she said,

"when can I come back home? When will you forgive me?"

"Azie, please—I am not sending you to Aunt Paulette's to punish you. Nani told you, this is for your own good." Then he turned quickly to Fanchon, not wanting Azalee to see the sadness in his eyes. "Take care of Azie," he said.

"I will try, Monsieur, but her care may not be in my hands."

Monsieur La Fontaine shook his head. He not only had Azalee to cope with during the last few days, he had trouble with Fanchon, too. She had insisted that this was not the time for Azalee to take a sea voyage; it would not be safe.

"Such nonsense," Pierre La Fontaine had said. "Azie's going down the coast and will never be out of sight of land. You cannot call that a sea voyage, Fanchon."

"But she will be at sea," Fanchon had said, "in many ways . . . she will be at sea."

But, if Pierre La Fontaine was not moved by Azalee's pleading, he wouldn't be touched by Fanchon's cryptic remarks. She was only trying to frighten him, because she, like Azalee, wanted to stay in New Orleans.

Now, standing on the dock, he watched the *Isabella* move slowly out of port. The ship passed a spit of land and was soon gone from sight. Gone, and so was his beautiful Azalee.

*   *   *

Azalee leaned against the ship's rail and started to cry. The spires and roofs of New Orleans were still visible, and she stayed on deck until the very last one disappeared from view. After that, she went below to her cabin.

Fanchon was struggling with the lock on one huge wardrobe trunk. "There is no place for all your clothes, Azie. I don't know where to put everything."

Azalee shrugged. "What difference does it make what I wear, Fanchon? There's no one here to see me."

Fanchon sighed. "That is true. But here, Azie, change into this cream wool dress. You are having dinner with the captain."

"I won't be long," Azalee told Fanchon when she left their cabin. "I'm sure that dinner on board the *Isabella* can't take more than fifteen minutes, and the food's probably terrible."

Azalee was surprised by the captain's cabin. It was large and comfortable, the walnut dining table was set with crystal and silver, and a decanter of wine was on the sideboard. The table was set for three, and the captain introduced his other guest. "This is my first mate, Roland Chevalier, Mademoiselle. I've asked him to dine with us."

Azalee looked at the ship's officer. He was a little older than most of the young men she knew in New Orleans—at least twenty-five—and very attractive. His light blue eyes were in surprising contrast to his dark hair and his skin, which was darkened by the sun. Suddenly, the trip to her Aunt Paulette's seemed less boring. "Monsieur Roland," she said, smiling, "are you also from New Orleans?"

"No, Mademoiselle, I am from France, from Paris."

"Paris!" Azalee was enchanted. Her father had had a few French visitors to his house, and she loved talking to them. They told her about another world, and, though New Orleans was her city, it wasn't Paris.

Captain Bercy smiled. Azalee looked better, he decided. He had known her since she was a child, and he was not happy that her father had chosen him to take his daughter into exile. Pierre La Fontaine had told him that his daughter was pining; that she had kept to her room and that she was hardly eating. But Captain Bercy watched her eat heartily of the sautéed fish, and was happy to see her eyes widen when the steward set a portion of puffy chocolate soufflé before her.

"Soufflé! On board ship!" she said. "I never thought we'd be eating like this."

"The British serve their men hardtack biscuits and salt pork," Roland Chevalier said, "but this is a ship from New Orleans, which is like a corner of France."

Azalee ate every bit of her soufflé and decided that she liked being on board the *Isabella*, after all. She would have to get off in three days, but for those three days she would enjoy herself.

After dinner, the first mate asked the captain if he might be excused and if Azalee would like to come up on deck with him.

"I would love to," she told him. "I've never been at sea before."

Azalee strolled about the deck with the first mate, and she felt as though she had never seen the moon so large and so magnificent. "It's wonderful being here," she exclaimed. "I never thought I'd like sailing so much."

Roland Chevalier stood close to her. "It's wonderful having you here," he said. "We hardly ever have women aboard the *Isabella*."

"I want to see everything. Will you take me all over the ship, Monsieur Chevalier?"

"My name is Roland, Mademoiselle, and I don't think the captain would like it if I took you all over the ship. And you wouldn't like it either, not in those clothes."

"I wish I had packed my father's riding breeches. Then I could have gone all over, even up there." She pointed to the rigging, where she could see a sailor balancing precariously in the crow's nest.

"I don't know what Captain Bercy would say, but I might be able to get some sailor's clothes for you tomorrow." He decided to ask the captain in the morning.

"It's irregular," Captain Bercy said, "but all right. Azalee's only a child, but quite a beautiful one, and she'll be less likely to give the men ideas if she's not wearing women's clothing."

Roland Chevalier smiled as he went about collecting dark blue sailor's pants, a striped blue and white jersey shirt, and a cap for Azalee. The captain might see her as a child, but, the night before, when he stood beside her at the ship's rail and smelled her perfume and saw the lustrous wave of her hair, he knew that she was no child. Besides, he had heard about her in New Orleans. She had danced with Jean Lafitte and enticed two young officers to take her riding into the bayous. She was definitely not a child.

"I feel wonderful," Azalee said, after she had changed her clothes and tucked her long hair snugly under the sailor's cap, "and comfortable. Now will you show me around the ship, Roland?"

Fanchon hovered close by. "I told your father not to send you on this ship," she said. "I told him that it was bad for you to be at sea."

"What could happen to me, Fanchon? There are no balls, no pirates, no horses, and no place to go riding. I'm perfectly safe."

Roland smiled. "As safe as you want to be, Mademoiselle."

Roland and Azalee walked around the deck of the ship. He showed her the galley where the meals were prepared, showed her the cargo hold, even showed her where his own small cabin was located. "This is where I sleep," he said. "Would you like to come in?"

Azalee backed into the narrow passageway. Roland couldn't have meant that. It was her wearing sailor's clothes that confused him. No man would invite a decent girl into his bedroom—not even aboard ship. "I think I'd rather climb the rigging," she said, and she ran up the stairs to the deck. Before he could stop her, she had climbed onto the ship's railing and, from there, had actually stepped on the rigging.

"Mademoiselle Azalee!" Roland Chevalier reached for her, but she moved another step higher and clung to the rigging.

Azalee felt the wind on her face, and looked down at the white wake of water rushing by. It was wonderful—she felt like a bird.

Fanchon stood below and spoke quietly to Azalee. "It is for things like this that your papa and grandmother sent you away from them. I did not think so, but perhaps they were right."

Azalee no longer felt wonderful. She had done it again; she had behaved recklessly. Moving carefully, she climbed down the rigging and allowed Roland Chevalier to lift her from the railing and place her back on the deck. Did his hands linger a minute longer than necessary around her waist? Probably her imagination.

"I'm sorry, Fanchon," she said. "It was the excitement of the waves and the water."

"There are other ways to find excitement on board ship," Roland Chevalier said softly.

"My Azalee has had quite enough excitement for one day," Fanchon said, stepping out of the shadows created by the setting sun. "Come, Azie."

Back in their cabin, Fanchon told Azalee not to change for dinner.

"But what will Captain Bercy say?"

"I think the captain understands that you are safer in that boy's outfit, Azie. In one of your gowns . . . well, these sailors are too quick to get ideas. I heard the way that Roland Chevalier spoke to you. I told your papa . . . you were safer in New Orleans."

"Are you worried about Roland?" Azalee asked. "He's just being polite. I'm safe on the *Isabella*. Don't be silly, Fanchon."

"Very well, I will not be silly," Fanchon said, "but I will watch out for my Azie all the same. I will do what Isabella would want me to do."

"*Isabella?* This ship?" she questioned.

"No. My Isabella, your mother. I feel her close to us. Perhaps because we are on the ship named for her, or perhaps because a spirit feels more free on sea than on land. The land cages a spirit, but at sea she is free to come to us."

Such talk! Azalee was glad to leave the tiny cabin and join the captain for dinner. He told her, with a smile, that Roland would be joining them again. *He thinks of me as a child,* Azalee realized, *and he's providing me with a playmate. But I'm not a child. I certainly didn't feel like a child when I danced with Johnny.* She did her best to push that thought from her mind, and she smiled at Roland Chevalier when he came in to the captain's cabin.

Captain Bercy told Azalee that the *Isabella* was about to change course. "The coast is too rocky here," he said. "We'll sail toward open waters. You'll really be at sea tonight, Azalee."

"Will there be anything special to see?" she asked.

"The stars," Roland said. "When you're in open waters they are really magnificent."

"Yes, yes. Go up on deck, both of you," the captain told them.

Azalee and Roland had walked around the deck of the *Isabella,* and now they leaned against the ship's railing.

"You're wonderful," Roland said, and he placed his arm around her shoulder. "I never knew a girl quite so wonderful, or quite so beautiful."

Azalee stiffened as Roland pulled her closer to him. "Roland, don't!" she said, sure that he would stop, simply because she wanted him to stop. That's the way it had always been with the young men she knew in New Orleans.

"You don't mean that, Azie," he said. "We can go below to my cabin."

"No!" Her voice was louder. "I *do* mean it!"

"New Orleans manners," Roland said. "You say no when you mean yes—"

"When Mademoiselle Azalee says no, she means *no!*" Fanchon stepped forward from the shadows. She held a large pistol in both hands, and it was pointed at Roland Chevalier.

Roland laughed. "It takes two hands for you just to hold that pistol, Mademoiselle Fanchon. You will need a third hand to pull the trigger. Let me have the pistol. You can't use it."

Fanchon's aim didn't waver. "This pistol was given to me by Isabella's father. He asked me to protect his daughter. I know that Isabella would want me to protect her daughter. Release Azie, Monsieur!"

"But I don't wish to release her, not just yet. You'll have to shoot me—if you have the courage . . ."

There was a loud report, and Azalee felt Roland release his hold on her. He clutched his shoulder and his eyes widened in surprise. "I didn't think you could do it," he whispered just before he slumped to the deck.

"Fanchon!" Azalee ran to her. "You've killed him!"

Fanchon looked with bewilderment at the pistol still in her hands. "But it wasn't me, Azie. I couldn't pull the trigger—"

It was then that they heard the sound of more gunfire.

"Ahoy, the *Isabella*," a shout came out of the night, "those were just warning shots. Heave to, or we'll blow you out of the water!"

"Fanchon," Azalee shouted, "look!"

Out of the blackness of sea and sky a British naval vessel came alongside the *Isabella*. Its white sails were bellied out by the wind and its cannons were pointed straight at the hull of Pierre La Fontaine's prize ship.

"Ahoy, the *Isabella*," the voice called again, "submit to a boarding party or we'll shoot!"

Members of the crew came running up on deck, Captain Bercy with them. "Go below," he shouted to Azalee and Fanchon, "go below! Where's my first mate? Where is the man?"

Azalee could only point to Roland, lying on the deck. "They've shot Mr. Chevalier," Captain Bercy shouted to his crew. "He may be dead."

"I'm not dead," Roland Chevalier groaned. "It's my shoulder, Captain."

Captain Bercy bent toward him. "Thank God for that," he said. Then he looked up at Azalee and Fanchon. "Ladies—please, go below. You'll be safer there."

"Come, Azie," Fanchon said, "we must go below."

"No," Azalee said, pulling away. "The *Isabella* is my father's ship—perhaps I can help the captain save her. You go below, Fanchon."

"I won't leave you," Fanchon told her.

"We're not armed," Azalee heard Captain Bercy call out. "We carry cargo, nothing more. We have no military supplies, no soldiers aboard—"

"Get ready to board," the shout came from the British warship.

Azalee saw British officers followed by eight or ten sailors come on board the *Isabella*.

"This is a civilian ship," Captain Bercy was shouting, "with a civilian crew. You have no right—"

"Our guns give us the right," one of the British officers shouted back. "You men," he instructed the British sailors, "you know what to do—step lively!"

The British sailors pulled pistols from their belts, and, moving quickly, they forced some of the *Isabella*'s crew to cross the plank that separated their ship from the British warship.

"Here's another," a British sailor shouted, as he came upon Azalee and Fanchon hiding in the shadows. "Come along now," he said, as he pointed his pistol and took Azalee roughly by the shoulder.

"Wait," Fanchon said, "stop!"

The sailor held his pistol to Azalee's head. "You better put that pistol down, woman," he told Fanchon, "unless you want to see this lad shot and thrown to the fish."

"Let me go," Azalee said, trying to get free. "You don't know who I am—"

"Cabin boy, by the look and sound of you. Never mind, you can be cabin boy aboard His Majesty's ship *George*. Stop that now," he said, shaking Azalee until she went limp. "Won't walk? I'll carry you!"

"Captain Bercy," Fanchon called out, "stop that man—he has Azie!"

The captain was struggling with two sailors, who held him back, his arms pinned to his sides. He saw the British sailor carry Azalee across the plank that separated the *George* and the *Isabella,* and he shouted, "Stop! Someone stop that man!"

A British officer laughed. "We'll give you your cabin boy back, Captain, after we've trained him to be a proper British sailor. Boarding party, back to the *George!* Captain, our guns are trained across your bow. Give us any trouble and we'll sink you. Then you'll never see your cabin boy or the rest of your crew again!"

Chapter 8

"HOIST SAIL!" THE COMMAND WAS SHOUTED ABOARD the *George*. "Move lively, there, we're too close to the American shore."

The crew of the *George* moved quickly, and soon the ship pulled away from the *Isabella* and was heading toward the open sea.

Azalee and some of the *Isabella*'s crew were huddled against a railing, guarded by British sailors.

"What is this?" Azalee asked. "What are they going to do to us?"

"We're impressed is what we are," one of the crew whispered to her. "Impressed into the British Navy—like it or not."

"You'll like it just fine," a British sailor said. "You'll take His Majesty's pay and eat His Majesty's hardtack same as the rest of us."

Azalee couldn't believe it. *"Impressed?"* she asked. "Americans in the British Navy? How could that happen?"

"They've got the guns, Miss. That's what counts. Who has the guns."

Azalee didn't understand. How could this have happened to her? And then she looked down and saw her sailor's clothes. They had impressed her—Azalee La Fontaine of New Orleans—into the British Navy, because they thought she was a boy!

She stood up just a little straighter. "You," she called out to one of the sailors who held a pistol. "Take me to your captain—at once!"

The sailor laughed. "Hear that? You sure it's the captain you want, boy? Won't First Lieutenant Braddock do as well? He can give you the flogging you seem to be aching for."

"You fool," Azalee shouted, "take me to your captain, or my father will kill you when he finds out what you've done to me."

"Father, is it? Who's your father, boy? The captain of the *Isabella?* He seemed pretty upset when we took you on board the *George.*"

"My father is Pierre La Fontaine of New Orleans," she said, "and I am no boy—"

"What's all the noise here?" one of the British officers asked the sailor. "Can't you keep these men quiet, Walton?"

"It's just this boy, Lieutenant Braddock, sir. Keeps asking to see the captain. Talks about his father. I don't think he's quite right up here, sir," he said, tapping his temple.

"He can work, can't he?" the officer asked. "He doesn't have to navigate the *George,* just serve the captain his meals on time and run a few errands. I suppose he's smart enough for that."

"Serve the captain his meals!" Azalee was furious. "I demand that you take me and our crew back to the *Isabella,* you . . . you kidnapper!"

"Kidnapper!" the British officer fumed. "You're young and I don't like to put the lash to a boy, but if you go on this way—"

"I am not a boy! How many times do I have to tell you that?"

"What do you call yourself, then?" the officer jeered. "A man?"

Azalee pulled off the cap under which she had hidden her long, dark hair. "I'm a girl—"

"What?" The officer took two steps back. "What are you doing here? What idiot brought a woman on board? This is a warship not a pleasure cruise. Who dared smuggle this woman on board?"

"He did," Azalee said, pointing at the sailor.

"Walton," the officer said, "how dare you? The captain will have you flogged for this."

"But I didn't know it was a girl, sir," Walton protested. "She was dressed in those clothes . . . like a boy, she was. I took her for the cabin boy, sir, and . . . and so did you."

"You," Lieutenant Braddock said, turning on Azalee. "What were you doing on board the *Isabella?*"

"The *Isabella* is my father's ship, and I had every right to be on board. But you don't have the right to force me and these men to stay on the *George*. We're Americans! Take me to your captain—now!"

Lieutenant Braddock stared at Azalee. He had heard about American women—heard that they were brave and that some of them even fought beside their men. But this was no woman—this was a young girl. He would have to let Captain Hammond handle this matter.

"Captain Hammond, sir," the lieutenant said when they had arrived at the captain's quarters, "there seems to have been some mistake—"

"Mistake?" The captain looked at the pretty girl dressed in sailor's clothing. "Which of my men had the audacity to smuggle his woman on board my ship? I'll have him court-martialed and then hanged!"

"I'm nobody's woman," Azalee said angrily. "I was a passenger on the *Isabella,* until I was dragged onto the *George*—"

"A passenger?" the captain said. "A fine passenger dressed like that. Does the captain of the *Isabella* always provide this kind of amusement for his crew? It's no wonder the *Isabella* was so easy to board."

"How dare you?" Azie could barely whisper those words, her throat was so constricted with anger. "I am Azalee La Fontaine, and my father is Pierre La Fontaine of New Orleans. He owns the *Isabella,* and I was on my way to Isle Sainte Marie—and now I demand that you take me back to the *Isabella*—"

"Demand!" the captain roared. "Who are you to demand anything?"

"I told you," Azalee said, from between clenched teeth. "I'm Azalee La Fontaine. And I insist that you take me and the men from the *Isabella* back to my father's ship!"

The captain looked at Azalee with astonishment.

This girl, who should have been weeping and begging for her life, was instead standing before him making outrageous demands. He admired her courage, and his anger diminished.

"It's not quite that simple, Miss . . . Miss—"

"La Fontaine," Lieutenant Braddock provided.

"Yes. Miss La Fontaine. We went to a great deal of trouble to track the *Isabella,* and we need those men on our ship. But you, Miss La Fontaine. This is a warship and we have no provisions for a woman."

Azalee sighed. "Then wouldn't it be simpler to let me leave?"

"Let you leave?" The captain gestured to the water outside the porthole. "We are at sea, Miss La Fontaine. I cannot put you off at the nearest wave. You are not a mermaid."

"Exactly," Azalee said. "That's why I want to go back to the *Isabella* with the rest of the *Isabella*'s crew."

"That's not possible," the captain said. "Lieutenant Braddock, you will arrange a cabin for Miss La Fontaine. Donaldson's cabin might do. Donaldson is my cabin boy," he explained to Azalee. "He was hoping to advance somewhat in rank, and he might have, too, if you had been the cabin boy we thought you were—"

"But, Captain," Azalee said, "I want to go back to the *Isabella.*"

"I'm sorry, Miss La Fontaine. I'm sure that you usually get exactly what you want, but this time you'll have to do what I want—which is to remain on board the *George,* until I can put you off at a convenient British port."

"Convenient?" Azalee asked. "Convenient for whom?"

"Why, Miss La Fontaine, convenient for me, of course."

Chapter 9

PIERRE LA FONTAINE WAS IN A RAGE. "WHAT DO you mean they boarded the *Isabella?*" he asked. "Where was the man on watch?"

"It was a fast British sloop," Captain Bercy explained, "and they were running without lights. We didn't know they were near until they were upon us. They had cannon, and there was nothing we could do—"

"Nothing you could do! And nothing you could do to stop them from taking Azalee?"

"They thought she was one of the sailors . . . a member of the crew."

"Why would they think that?"

"She was dressed like a sailor," the captain said.

"What! Fanchon, how could you permit this?"

"It was safer for Azie to wear boys' clothes on that ship," Fanchon said. "I told you, Monsieur La Fontaine. I told you there would be danger if you sent her to sea."

"I didn't send her to sea," Pierre La Fontaine

shouted. "I was sending her to my sister's home in Isle Sainte Marie. Don't blame this disaster on me, Fanchon."

But he didn't need Fanchon to blame him, he blamed himself. He should have sailed on the *Isabella* with Azalee. That would have been the only way of keeping her safe. "We must find her," he said. "We must get her back."

"Even if we find the *George*," Captain Bercy said, "there is no way an unarmed merchant ship can board a British warship. They will either blow us out of the water, or they'll impress more of our crew."

"Lafitte," Pierre La Fontaine said. "I'll go to Lafitte—he'll find the *George*. He'll get Azalee back, and then he'll blow the *George* out of the water!"

"You'll ask that pirate for help?" Captain Bercy said.

"I'd ask the devil for help, if it would mean getting Azalee back."

Pierre La Fontaine prepared for his ride to Barataria Bay. Captain Corday offered to send men from the New Orleans Regiment with him, but Azalee's father refused his help.

"She's my daughter, and I will do what is necessary," he said to the captain. "Besides, if I arrive with soldiers, Lafitte may feel that we're coming to attack him—and I need his help."

"A pirate's help?" Captain Corday said.

"Can you get my daughter back?" Pierre La Fontaine asked.

"No."

"Then I will be grateful for a pirate's help."

Pierre La Fontaine boarded another one of his ships, the *Charlotte*. It would take him part of the way to Barataria Bay, but the last part of the journey he would have to do on horseback.

The *Charlotte* hugged the coast, never sailing out of sight of land and traveling only by day. He kept thinking of Azalee on board the *George*. What were they doing to her? How were they treating her?

Finally, the ship docked at Pointe La Touraine and Pierre started his ride across the peninsula that separated him from Barataria Bay. He would have whipped his horse to go faster, except that he was afraid that the animal would drop from exhaustion, leaving him without a mount.

The horse rested when they rode the skiffs that took them across the small bodies of water that dotted the peninsula. Pierre La Fontaine stood on the various flat-bottomed skiffs, looking toward the opposite shore. *Azalee, Azalee. What is happening to my Azalee?*

When he arrived at Barataria Bay, he had to charter a boat to take him to Grand Terre Island—Jean Lafitte's stronghold—and none of the boat owners were willing to make the trip.

"Jean Lafitte doesn't like company," one man told him.

"The last captain who sailed to Grand Terre didn't come back," another said.

Pierre La Fontaine was in despair. He could see Grand Terre Island, but he couldn't get to it. Finally, he thought of a way.

"I want to buy your boat," he said to a man with a small sailing ship. The man named his price. "I'll pay that," Pierre La Fontaine said, "if you take me to Grand Terre Island."

"I've changed my mind," the man said. "I don't want to sell my boat, after all."

No amount of money could persuade the man, and Pierre La Fontaine spent another anguished afternoon looking at Grand Terre Island—still so near, and yet so far.

The next day a man approached him. "I understand you wish to go to Grand Terre Island, Monsieur."

"Yes, yes—will you take me?"

"Are you Pierre La Fontaine?"

"Yes. How did you know?"

"Captain Lafitte sent me. He heard that there was a man here claiming that he had been invited to visit Jean Lafitte, but Captain Lafitte said that he had invited a man and his daughter. Is your daughter here, Monsieur?"

"That's why I want to see Captain Lafitte. It's about my daughter. I need his help."

The man grinned. "Not too many fathers ask for Jean Lafitte's help with their daughters, Monsieur, but, as you are Pierre La Fontaine, I will take you to Grand Terre Island."

Finally, Pierre La Fontaine boarded a boat that would take him to Grand Terre Island. When he arrived, he was greeted by both Jean Lafitte and John Trent.

"But the charming Mademoiselle Azalee," Jean Lafitte said, "I was hoping to see her with you. Is she well?"

"It's about Azalee that I've come," Pierre La Fontaine said. And he told them about Azalee's adventure in the bayous and his subsequent decision to send her out of New Orleans by way of the *Isabella*. "I should never have sent her with only Fanchon," he said. "I should have gone with her myself."

Lafitte shrugged. "But I still don't understand. It is not like the British to take women prisoners aboard a warship."

"They didn't know she was a woman," Pierre La Fontaine revealed. "She was dressed in sailors' clothes."

Lafitte laughed loudly. "She has courage, that daughter of yours, and imagination—"

"Too much courage and too much imagination," Johnny said angrily.

It seemed to Johnny that he had spent every waking hour—and many of his sleeping ones, too—thinking and dreaming about Azalee La Fontaine.

He had forced himself not to call on her after their one dance at the ball, because she had seemed all too willing to dance with Jean Lafitte. He could never forget how warm and sweet her body had felt next to his, but, when he saw her in Lafitte's arms, he was sure that she enjoyed making all men fall in love with her. He hadn't meant anything to her—and he didn't want to give her another chance to hurt him with her flirtatious ways.

But now—now she was in the hands of the enemy. And, as angry as he was with her, he wanted to be the one to save her.

"We'll sail at once," he said to Lafitte and Pierre La Fontaine.

Lafitte's eyebrows went up in amazement. "At once? We must wait for the tide. Besides, what would your General Jackson say to my risking a ship just to save one silly girl?"

"She's not a silly girl," Pierre La Fontaine roared. "She's my daughter! Besides, Lafitte's ships were supposed to protect our ships from the British. Where were they the night the *George* attacked the *Isabella?*"

"We don't have as many ships as the British," Lafitte explained calmly.

"But Monsieur La Fontaine is right," Johnny said. "We should have protected the *Isabella.*"

"And we would have," Jean Lafitte said, amused at Johnny Trent's very evident concern, "if we had known that Mademoiselle Azalee was aboard. But now it is clearly our duty to rescue her. I will ready one of my ships, and we'll sail as soon as possible.

"Meanwhile, can you get word to General Jackson, Monsieur La Fontaine, that Lieutenant Trent and I are going after the *George?*"

"But I'd like to sail with you," Pierre La Fontaine said.

"It's more important for you to see General Jackson. You must tell him to hold off any further action on this coast until he hears from us," Lafitte said. "I can't go after the *George* unless you give me your word that you'll see the general."

"You have my word," Pierre La Fontaine said.

"Then as soon as one of my ships is properly armed, we'll go hunting—for the *George*."

"And for Azalee . . ." Pierre La Fontaine and Johnny Trent said at the same time.

Jean Lafitte looked at the two men. "Of course," he said, smiling at them, "for Azalee."

Chapter 10

Wednesday, aboard the George: I AM A PRISONER aboard a British warship. I have been so bored that I asked Captain Hammond for paper, a pen, and a pot of ink. There's hardly anyone on board who will talk to me, and, rather than talk to myself, like some fool, I have decided to record my impressions in this diary. When I'm rescued, I'll be able to tell everyone exactly what happened—that is, *if* I'm rescued, and *if* I ever see New Orleans again.

Captain Hammond is not at all like Captain Bercy (and I don't care if he reads this diary and sees what I've written about him!). Captain Bercy was so kind. He wanted me to enjoy my trip on the *Isabella,* and he let me wander all over the ship. Captain Hammond is nothing like that. He expects me to stay in my cabin *all* the time. I am allowed a short walk on deck after lunch, and then once again before dinner, but I have to be accompanied by Lieutenant Braddock or one of the other officers, and they barely talk to me. Braddock looks grim when we go for our walk, and I'm just as glad to go back to my cabin when he says, "Had enough air for the day, Miss La Fontaine?"

I may not have had enough air, but I've had enough of him, so I say, "Yes, thank you very much, Lieutenant Braddock," and then he escorts me back to my cabin.

More tomorrow. The bell had just rung for dinner, and the captain demands promptness. "Promptness is the courtesy of kings, Miss La Fontaine," he says, "and if you cannot be prompt, you will just have to miss dinner."

Well!

Thursday, aboard the George: When I said I was a prisoner on this ship, I meant just that. My cabin door is locked and there is a sailor always posted right outside. Captain Hammond says that's because it's been months since his crew has seen a "pretty young lady like you, Miss La Fontaine." But if no one can come in, I also cannot get out. I've tried, but the guard at the door told me that the captain would have him flogged, if he let me go wandering off.

So here I am, trapped in this tiny cabin, with absolutely nothing to do and no one to talk to.

All I have to wear are two sailor outfits from Captain Hammond's cabin boy, Donaldson, and one outfit is exactly like the other.

I miss my clothes! I liked wearing sailors' clothes on the *Isabella* and Papa's breeches when I went riding, but I also liked my dresses. I'd give anything to be wearing one right now.

Friday, aboard the George: Donaldson, the cabin boy, brings me breakfast and lunch. How I long for New Orleans cooking. Breakfast here is this thick, mushy stuff—some kind of oatmeal, which Donaldson calls *porridge*—and awful, strong tea. Lunch is of cold meat, and, when I can't identify it, I don't eat it.

I have dinner every evening with Captain Hammond and his officers. The food isn't much better, except that it is hot. I remember hearing Papa make remarks about English cooking, and now I understand him. Captain Hammond does give me a drop or two of wine, but never more than that, and he says the same thing every evening. "I'm sure your father wouldn't mind if you had a drop of claret, Miss La Fontaine. Awfully good for the digestion."

I look down at my plate when he says that, not because of the wine, but because I can hardly bear to think of Papa. He must be frantic about me. He can't know that I'm safe and unharmed, and I can imagine how worried he must be. I miss him so terribly, terribly much.

Saturday, and still aboard the George: I've tried very hard not to spend too much time thinking about Papa, Nani Charlotte, and Fanchon. If I do, I'll never stop crying, and I don't want these Englishmen to see how lonely and homesick and *scared* I really am.

I must act brave, no matter how I feel—it's the way Papa would want me to behave. But I am frightened. How long will I have to stay on this ship? Where will they put me off? Captain Hammond says he will find a British port for me, but where? And what will they do to me there? Does a British port mean prison? I don't know what will happen to me.

I'd better end before this page dissolves from my tears.

Sunday, aboard the George: I was allowed out of my cabin this morning to attend services with the rest of the ship's company. Captain Hammond stood on the bridge and read a part of the Bible which goes something like, "Your sea is so big, Lord, and I am so small," and I felt especially small when I looked around me.

The *George* has a large crew, and, when I noticed the way some of the men looked at me, I was glad that Captain Hammond has made me stay in my cabin. These men are not like the crew of the *Isabella*—they are the enemy. It doesn't matter to anyone on the *George* that I am Mademoiselle Azalee La Fontaine of New Orleans. To them, I am just another prisoner, and I shiver when I think of what might have happened had Captain Hammond not protected me.

I saw some the crew from the *Isabella,* but I couldn't talk to them. We were kept far apart during morning services. Imagine being forced into the enemy's navy. What will happen if the *George* goes into battle against an American ship? Will the Americans on the *George* be expected to fight against their own people? No man from the *Isabella* would ever shoot another American, I'm sure of that.

Monday, aboard the George: Donaldson finally spoke to me. He was so angry that I wasn't a real cabin boy that for days he would just put down my breakfast or lunch tray and leave without a word. But today he answered my "good morning" with a "morning, Miss," and that was a lot more pleasant.

When Donaldson came with lunch, I asked him why it was so important for him not to be a cabin boy any longer. When he told me something about his life, I could understand why he was so disappointed that I was a girl and not a cabin boy.

Donaldson works from four in the morning till way past midnight. He runs errands, serves meals, and works in the galley. He's always running and hardly sleeps, but, when another cabin boy is found, he will be made a junior officer.

I told him I couldn't understand why someone who was meant to be an officer had to go through this wretched cabin boy business. He explained that it was because his mother was a widow and didn't have enough money to buy him a commission in the navy, so he had to do it the hard way.

I didn't understand what a "commission" was. He said that after a certain amount of schooling—and if you knew important people—you could buy yourself a position in the British Navy or Army.

I don't think it's like that in the American Army. I'm

sure that Lieutenant John Trent was made an officer because he was brave, not because he was rich.

Johnny Trent. When I close my eyes, I can see us dancing together, and I can remember the way he made me feel. Does he know what has happened to me? And does he care?

Tuesday, aboard the George: Donaldson and I are friends now. He told me his first name—it's Stuart. When he brought in that awful porridge, I told him about the breakfasts we have in New Orleans: fresh crescent rolls, sweet butter, three kinds of jam, and hot coffee with frothy, hot milk. Stuart smiled. It sounded so wonderful compared to the food on the *George,* I thought he didn't believe me.

But, when he brought my lunch, he brought some of the food that Captain Hammond eats for breakfast— fine white rolls and orange marmalade. I asked Stuart why he hadn't brought such food before, and he said that Captain Hammond had ordered that I be served the same breakfast the crew eats. Something about "teaching that young lady a lesson," Stuart said.

I can't imagine anyone in New Orleans treating a guest—even an uninvited guest—so meanly. I can't even imagine an American treating someone like that. Not that I know any real Americans—except for Johnny Trent. Johnny—he wasn't really nice at all. That dance didn't mean a thing to him. The way he held me . . . he probably dances that way with all girls. I hate men who flirt! I really do!

*   *   *

Wednesday, aboard the George: Since I've been on the *George,* I've felt more like an American than I ever have before. Until now, I've just thought of myself as someone from New Orleans. And now I feel like an American. Oh, how I wish I could get back there—to New Orleans, to America.

Papa, when are you going to come and get me? When can I go home?

Thursday, aboard the George: I think this may be the last time I write in this diary. Stuart just came in with my lunch and said that an approaching ship has been sighted.

"American?" I asked Stuart.

"Sorry, Miss," he said. "It's flying a flag that has a castle on it with a crown on top. That's the *Corsair,* one of Jean Lafitte's ships. He's a pirate. Captain Hammond has done business with him before."

My heart is pounding. Maybe Captain Hammond doesn't know that Jean Lafitte has gone over to the Americans. Jean Lafitte is coming—he's coming to rescue me!

"I've never seen a pirate before," I told Stuart. "Do you think I could go up on deck to get a look at him?"

"They won't let you on deck, Miss," Stuart said, "but let me open this porthole for you. You'll be able to get a glimpse of him through here."

Stuart has left and I'm kneeling on the bunk bed and looking through the porthole. There it is—the most beautiful ship I've ever seen—coming toward us. I can see the flag with the castle on it. That must be the castle Jean Lafitte asked me to visit.

Now . . . now I can see Lafitte. Captain Hammond is letting him on board with some of his men. And there, right beside him, is Johnny Trent. He's come to rescue me!

Johnny, you *do* care. You must or you wouldn't risk your life to save mine!

Chapter 11

"SHOULDN'T WE BE FLYING THE AMERICAN FLAG?" Johnny asked Lafitte, when they finally spotted the *George* in the distance.

"It will be more of a surprise if we go in under my flag. The captain doesn't know that I've come over to the American side."

Johnny Trent preferred fighting under his own flag, but that wasn't important right now. The important thing was rescuing Azalee. Jean Lafitte was right. They would be welcome aboard the *George* flying Lafitte's colors.

The British captain raised his eyebrows at the number of men that suddenly surrounded him. "You've brought a lot of people with you, Captain Lafitte, for a friendly visit. Even an American Army officer, I see."

"Not so friendly," Lafitte said, as he raised his right hand, signaling the men on the *Corsair*. Captain Hammond saw the cannons move into position, until they were trained on the *George*. At the same time, another flag was hauled up the mast—the flag of the United States of America.

"But you are on *our* side, Lafitte?" Captain Hammond asked.

"I was, once," Lafitte answered, "and then I realized that at heart I'm an American patriot."

"A patriot," Hammond said bitterly, "a scoundrel and a thief."

"A scoundrel whose guns are pointed at your ship," Lafitte said. "Speak more softly, Captain, or I'll blow you out of the water."

"If that's what you wanted, you could have done it already. What have you really come for, Lafitte?"

"We have come for Azalee La Fontaine," Johnny said impatiently. "Where is she?"

"Johnny, Johnny—over here . . ." Azalee called from the porthole in her cabin.

Johnny turned. "Azalee," he said.

Captain Hammond looked at him in disbelief. "You've come after the *George* and risked your own ship, just for a girl?"

"You would have done better to have left her on the *Isabella,* Captain Hammond," Lafitte said.

"I would have been happy to have left her on the *Isabella,* but we didn't know that she was a girl until she arrived on board."

"Enough of this talk," Johnny said, anxious to have Azalee safe again. "I want to locate Mademoiselle La Fontaine."

"Relax, Lieutenant," Captain Hammond said. "She's right down below in one of the cabins."

Johnny had heard enough. He ran across the deck and down the stairs leading to the cabins.

"Johnny, Johnny," Azalee called, as she hammered on the cabin door from within.

Johnny turned the doorknob and realized that the cabin door was locked.

"I'll get the key, sir," the British sailor who was guarding Azalee said.

"Never mind," Johnny told him. "Azalee—stand away from the door." He put his shoulder to the door and heaved against it until it crashed open.

"Azalee . . ." She was in his arms then, sobbing, weeping, her sweet body pressed against his. He held her tightly to him; he would never let her go, never.

Azalee clung to him. "Johnny," she said, "you came for me."

"You knew I would," he said, his lips against her dark hair, "you knew I would . . ."

"Lieutenant Trent," Jean Lafitte called from above, "Lieutenant Trent—"

"Yes," Johnny shouted, "we're coming." His arm around Azalee, the two of them went up on deck.

"Mademoiselle La Fontaine," Lafitte said, "you're all right? No one harmed you?"

"I'm all right," Azalee said, doing her best to steady her voice.

"Then we must get back to the *Corsair*. Lieutenant—"

"Wait!" Azalee pulled away from Johnny. "There are men here from the *Isabella*. You can't leave them—they're Americans."

Johnny pulled her to him again. He wanted to kiss her. "That's my girl," he whispered. Then he turned toward the sailors on the deck. "The men from the *Isabella*," he shouted, "step forward."

The British tried to hold them back, but Lafitte's men moved forward with pistols and sabers, and the Americans gathered quickly around Azalee.

Lafitte got Azalee and the others into the longboat first, and then he and Johnny followed. "*Au 'voir*, Captain Hammond," Lafitte said, as they pulled away from the *George*, "perhaps we shall meet again."

"I hope so, Captain Pirate," the British captain said. "We will know you now—no matter which flag you're flying."

Azalee looked back at the *George*, as the men rowed toward the *Corsair*. "Is it safe?" she asked. "Won't they shoot at us?"

"Not with the guns of the *Corsair* aimed at their hull. We've won this engagement, Mademoiselle, and without bloodshed. That is most unusual."

"You won't shoot at the *George* once we get back to the *Corsair?*" Johnny asked Lafitte.

"In ten minutes they'll have their guns in position— and they have larger cannon and more of them. The only way to attack the *George* is by surprise, not to hand them our calling card, as we just did. Besides, we've accomplished our mission. We have rescued Mademoiselle La Fontaine."

"Captain Lafitte," Azalee said, "I was so frightened. Thank you for coming for me."

Johnny saw that Azalee was smiling at the pirate captain. *There she goes again. She doesn't have to be so all-fired grateful to the man! One minute she's in my arms thanking me, and now she looks as if she's ready to thank Lafitte the same way.*

Azalee was grateful. Johnny had come for her, but he had come in Lafitte's ship, so she said once again, "I do thank you, Captain, and I'm sure my father will thank you as well."

"You can thank me by being my guest on Grand Terre Island, Mademoiselle. Do you remember? I invited you on the night of the ball. Besides, you look a little tired, perhaps a little feverish."

"I remember," she said, "but I must get back to New Orleans. My father must be frantic."

"He was frantic," Lafitte told her, "but we'll send a message with the *Isabella*'s crew. They'll let your father know that you're safe."

The longboat pulled up beside the *Corsair,* and Azalee and the others climbed the ladder to the deck of the ship. Lafitte's orders were quick and crisp, and the *Corsair* moved rapidly away from the *George.*

Azalee could see that the British ship was not readying its guns. Captain Hammond knew that the *Corsair* would move quickly out of range, but his voice carried over the short distance between the two ships. "I will see you soon, Lafitte," he said.

"I look forward to the meeting, Captain," Lafitte replied.

Azalee began to tremble when she was in Jean Lafitte's cabin. She was shaking with a fever.

Johnny pulled a down quilt off the captain's bunk and wrapped her in it. "You're a little fool, Azie. You take terrible chances with your life, and you expect others to get you out of trouble."

Azalee didn't have the strength to answer him. Though the tone of his voice told her that he cared about her, still he was suddenly angry and she didn't know why.

"Brandy," Jean Lafitte said, when he came into his cabin and saw Azalee wrapped in a quilt and still shaking. "You need some brandy."

He poured an inch of amber-colored liquid into a crystal glass that was etched with a twining rose in full bloom. "Drink this," Lafitte said.

Johnny took the brandy glass from Lafitte. "I'll do it," he said brusquely, and he held the glass to Azalee's lips.

The brandy warmed her, and the presence of the two men made her feel safe. She hadn't meant to, but she couldn't help it—she was falling asleep.

Azalee felt someone wrap the quilt more tightly about her, and then someone—she didn't have the strength to open her eyes to see who—picked her up and put her on the captain's bunk. "Johnny," she thought she murmured, *"Johnny . . ."* And then she didn't think about anything.

Azalee remained in a heavy, feverish sleep until the *Corsair* arrived at Grand Terre Island.

Someone picked her up and carried her from the ship to the house. She opened her eyes long enough to see that it was Johnny. Then she fell asleep once again. Her sleep wasn't deep, and it was punctuated by dreams of she and Johnny dancing together.

The next time Azalee woke up it was morning, and she felt better. She looked around and saw that she was in the most beautiful room she had ever seen. The walls were covered in cream-colored silk patterned with entwining yellow roses. A large mirror, set in a gilt frame, was at the far end of the room, and the rugs were cream, with the same yellow roses twisting their way around the border. The sheets were fine linen, and the pillow slips were finished with cascades of lace.

I wish Nani Charlotte could see this, Azalee thought, as she touched the lace. Then she sat up in bed—she was naked! Who had taken off her clothes? Lafitte? Johnny? She saw a white silk dressing gown on top of the cover, and she put it on before she tugged at the embroidered bellpull that hung beside the bed.

Her ring was answered almost immediately by a smiling girl carrying a breakfast tray. "Good morning, Mademoiselle. My name is Yvonne. Would you like some breakfast?"

Azalee looked at the small, dark, pretty girl. "Did you, by any chance . . . did you undress me last night, Yvonne?" she asked her.

Yvonne nodded. "Yes, Mademoiselle, but it wasn't last night. It was the day before that. You slept over a day. Do you feel better now?"

"Oh, yes. A lot better now," Azalee said, and she

looked at the tray Yvonne carried. A porcelain pot held steaming black coffee, and the pitcher beside it was filled with hot milk, whipped to a froth.

"Mademoiselle," Yvonne said, "if you like, I'll run a bath for you after breakfast."

"I'd like that very much. I just wish I had something to wear after my bath—something besides that cabin boy uniform."

Yvonne went to the large oak closet at the far end of the room and opened the doors wide. "Captain Lafitte said he hoped you'd find something here you might like to wear."

Azalee pushed the tray away and got out of bed. She looked at the dresses hanging in the wardrobe. They were wonderful! There was a green silk moiré piped in white velvet, and a peach taffeta with tiny heart-shaped buttons. There was an ivory satin dress with pink ribbons and a lavender velvet with huge fan-shaped sleeves. They were marvelous clothes—the kind of clothes that Nani Charlotte and Fanchon told her could only be worn by a woman after she was married. And there wasn't a white dress in the entire closet.

It was later, when she was trying on the gowns, that Azalee remembered her father's words. Who had these dresses belonged to? Were the women they were meant for now lying on the ocean floor? Azalee took off the ivory satin dress and put on Stuart Donaldson's cabin boy uniform.

Jean Lafitte and Johnny Trent were waiting for her when she came downstairs a little later.

"I'm sorry, Mademoiselle," Lafitte said. "I thought you might like one of those dresses."

"I liked them all," Azalee said, "but I couldn't wear them. I'm sorry, Captain, but I don't know who they belonged to."

"They belong to me," Lafitte told her, "or to you, if you like them."

"I mean before . . . Who did they belong to *before*? Where did they come from?"

"I ordered them for you, Mademoiselle, right after we met. You remember that I invited you to Grand Terre Island? I hoped you would come, and I wanted to be prepared should you visit me."

What a story, Johnny thought, shaking his head in disbelief. How he wished he didn't have to serve with Lafitte on patrol duty. But it was General Jackson's orders, and there was nothing he could do about it.

"But . . . but if I had planned to visit you, I would have brought my own clothes . . ."

"Sometimes things happen without plan—as it just did. You came, but your clothes are in New Orleans. Did the dresses fit?"

Azalee was enchanted. "They fit beautifully, and they are beautiful—every one of them. I'm going right back upstairs and change."

Did she really believe him? Johnny wondered. She couldn't have. Azalee was no fool. But it was clear that she wanted to believe Lafitte, wanted to believe him because she liked the man—maybe even was falling in love with him.

He hated to think of her wearing clothes that the

pirate had stolen. "You may as well stay in what you're wearing," he said. "I've gotten used to seeing you in that outfit. Probably suits you better than a bunch of fancy folderols."

"Wait until you see Mademoiselle Azalee in those fancy folderols, as you call them," Lafitte said. "You'll see that they suit her very well."

Azalee ran up the stairs, taking them two at a time.

"Look, Captain," Johnny said, "we've got to get Azalee back to New Orleans. She'll be safe there."

"Safe?" Lafitte said. "You don't think the British would attack Grand Terre? We're a fortress here."

"It's not the British I'm thinking of," Johnny said, angrily.

"I know," Lafitte said smoothly. "But remember, Lieutenant—all's fair in love and war."

"She's just a child."

"Is she?" Lafitte turned to the staircase, and the two men saw Azalee come down slowly, dressed in an ivory satin gown that made her skin glow.

"You look lovely, Mademoiselle," Lafitte said, "just as I knew you would."

She did look lovely, Johnny thought. Lovely, and certainly grown up enough—for anything. He hated the way the pirate looked at her, and he hated the way Azalee smiled right back at him. "You looked better in that sailor's uniform," he said furiously. "Besides, you'll have to change back. I'm taking you to New Orleans."

"Not so quickly," Lafitte said. "Have you forgotten, Lieutenant? We're under orders to wait until

General Jackson sends us word as to where he wants us to mass our ships. You can't leave now, and we certainly cannot allow Mademoiselle Azalee to ride back to New Orleans without an escort."

"But Papa—" Azalee began.

"He knows you're safe," Lafitte told her. "We sent word with the men from the *Isabella.*"

"If you're sure . . ." Azalee said.

"Quite sure," Lafitte answered. "Now, let me show you around my home."

He offered Azalee his arm and she took it, and, as she walked past Johnny, her satin gown brushed against his legs. *He looks like a thundercloud,* Azalee thought. *Why does he always have to be so angry with me? He might just as well have said that I looked good in this gown.* She smiled at Lafitte, and thought that Johnny Trent could certainly take a few lessons from him on how to treat a lady!

Chapter 12

THE NEXT FEW DAYS WERE ENCHANTED ONES FOR Azalee. Jean Lafitte had created his own world on Grand Terre Island, and it was a world of beauty.

A glass greenhouse housed flowers from all over the world. There were tiny green orchids that looked like butterflies on the wing and giant, striped tiger lilies from the jungles of Brazil. A conservatory, also roofed in glass, was filled with birds—bright green parrots from the Amazon and pure white macaws from Mexico.

Everywhere she looked Azalee saw something wonderful. She enjoyed wandering between the greenhouse and the conservatory, not sure which she admired most—the brightly colored flowers or the vividly plumed birds.

"You look mighty silly wandering around in that fancy dress," Johnny said one day as a blue and yellow parrot pecked at the seeds Azalee held in the palm of her hand.

Azalee looked down at the apricot silk gown with the flutter of ribbons on each sleeve. She knew the dress was wonderful and that she looked wonderful in it. "I don't think you'd like me no matter what I was wearing, Lieutenant." Azalee spoke lightly, but she hoped he would understand what she really meant: *Treat me the way you did the day you rescued me from the* George.

She was standing so close to him that he found it hard to breathe, but it didn't mean a thing, he knew that. She was just flirting. One minute she was playing up to him, and the next she'd do the same thing with Lafitte. He wished he could flirt back, but he didn't know how. He could only answer her honestly.

"I like you well enough," he said, his topaz eyes flashing golden sparks, "and, if we were in Tennessee . . ."

"Yes?" Azalee whispered. "What would happen if we were in Tennessee?"

He wanted to take her in his arms, crush her to him, show her how men and women behaved where he came from. But that's probably what she was waiting for—and then she'd laugh at him. He stepped back from her. "Never mind," he said. "This isn't Tennessee. Girls don't act like you do in Tennessee."

Azalee took a step closer to him. "Just how would you have me act, Lieutenant? What would you like me to do?"

"It's more what I'd like you *not* to do—not that it's any of my business. It's your father's problem, and I pity the man."

"Let's pretend for just a minute that it is your

business," Azalee said softly. "What would you like me not to do?"

"I'd like it if you didn't go around dressed in a sailor's clothes and getting impressed into the British Navy. And I'd like not to have to go around rescuing you—I have more important things to do, like fighting a war . . . and, most of all, I'd like you not to carry on with Captain Lafitte."

"Me, carry on? I do no such thing! What do you mean, *carry on?*"

"You're wearing the clothes he gave you, aren't you? And you're always thanking him for one thing or another. And the way you make a fuss over everything he says, it's enough to make a man sick."

"It doesn't make Captain Lafitte sick," Azalee lashed out, "and he's every bit as much of a man as you are!"

Johnny took her by the shoulders and shook her. "Don't worry about my being a man," he said. "What you should think about is how you can grow up and become a woman."

"I am a woman!"

"You're a spoiled child—that's all you are—used to getting your own way."

Azalee broke free of him. She wanted to cry, but she held back the tears. "You're horrible," she said, "mean and horrible. Of course, I'm nice to Captain Lafitte—he's nice to me. All you do is criticize. You don't like what I wear, you don't like what I say, you don't like anything about me!"

Johnny looked at Azalee and wished he could get

the words out—wished he could say, *I like you too much; that's the trouble*. But he couldn't say that to her, because no matter how much he cared for her, she *was* spoiled, *was* used to getting her own way, and there was no room in his life for a girl like that. But he knew that he would miss her all his life long, knew that he'd never find a girl he could love as much as he loved and longed for Azalee.

Finally, he did say, "I wish I had never gone to the Duval house the night of that ball, Azalee, and I wish I had never asked you to dance. *I wish I had never met you!*"

Azalee burst into tears, and then she hated herself for letting him see her cry. She didn't want him to know how she felt about him, didn't want him to know how he had hurt her. "Just forget that you did meet me," she said through her tears, "and I'll certainly forget that I ever met you. That shouldn't be too hard for either one of us." Then she ran out of the conservatory.

There! She had gotten in the last word. She was glad about that, but when she was in her room, she couldn't stop crying. *I'll never forget him,* she thought, *never! But I may die of the pain of remembering what he just said to me.*

When Johnny heard the door of the conservatory open once again, he hoped she had come back. Somehow, he couldn't go to her—he still believed that she would laugh if she knew how much he loved her. He only knew his own heart, he thought unhappily, and he wasn't at all sure of hers.

But it wasn't Azalee, it was Jean Lafitte. "Lover's quarrel?" Lafitte asked.

"Azalee isn't interested in me," the words burst out of Johnny, though he hated showing Lafitte how much he really cared about Azalee. "I'm just one more man for her to flirt with—one more man that she can drive crazy. She's a spoiled child. I don't mean a thing to her."

"If I were sure of that," Lafitte said, "I'd work harder to get her interested in me."

Johnny looked at him. Did the pirate think he would ever let him touch Azalee? He'd kill him first. "Interested? What do you mean?" he asked, a threat clearly in his voice.

"I wouldn't harm her," Lafitte said. "I would ask her to be my wife."

"Azalee? A pirate's wife?"

"No, the wife of a gentleman, which is what I'll be after this war is over, thanks to your General Jackson. That's what I'd do. I'd ask your Azalee to marry me."

"She's not *my* Azalee," Johnny said.

"No? Are you sure? Then maybe I *will* ask her to be Madame Jean Lafitte."

Johnny winced, but he hoped his words masked his feelings. "Go ahead! Go ahead and ask her. It doesn't mean anything to me. Why not do it now, while she's under your roof, wearing your clothes?"

"Now? Certainly not," Lafitte said. "I will ask Mademoiselle Azalee La Fontaine to be my wife when I am a gentleman. But now we are at war, Lieutenant, and we have received word. We should be out patrolling the coast. After all, we don't want any more American ships attacked by the British."

Johnny forced himself back under control. "I'm ready to leave when you are," he said.

"Tonight, then, with the tide." Lafitte looked at Johnny and smiled. "Won't you be a little sorry to leave Mademoiselle Azalee, Lieutenant?"

"It will be a relief," Johnny said bitterly. He wanted to get away from her—and he wanted to get Lafitte away from her, too.

After dinner that night, Lafitte told Azalee that he and Lieutenant Trent would be sailing on the *Corsair* in an hour. "You'll be safe here," he said, "and when we return, one of us will ride with you to New Orleans."

Azalee looked around the beautiful dining room. It wouldn't be so wonderful remaining in this huge house with Johnny gone. "Can't I go with you?" she asked Lafitte. "I still have Stuart Donaldson's clothes. I could wear them on the *Corsair.*"

Johnny had been toying with his dessert, and now he let his spoon bang against his plate. "Typical!" he said, almost shouting. "That's just typical, Azalee. You're only happy when you're in danger!" He stood up, pushing his chair back so hard that it fell against the marble floor, and he stormed out of the dining room.

"What did I do?" Azalee asked and ran out of the room, too.

Lafitte poured himself a glass of brandy and raised

his glass to one of the paintings that hung on the dining room wall. It was a portrait of a beautiful woman wearing a dark red velvet gown, the color of the dress in perfect contrast to her diamond necklace. Lafitte remembered the ship from which he had plucked the painting and the necklace, and the dresses that were meant for a woman who waited in vain for them. He had hung the painting in his dining room, because he hoped that one day he would have a lady like that for his wife.

That red gown was the only one he hadn't given to Azalee. He was afraid that she might recognize it, if she so much as glanced at the portrait. But she had accepted the other dresses and she believed that the clothes were made especially for her. How naive, how charming, and how beautiful she was. The young lieutenant might love her and she might love him, but they were children. They didn't know what to do about their love. Besides, love wasn't all that important. If Azalee La Fontaine married him, she could have everything he owned, and he would make up another story about that diamond necklace.

"I have your necklace, my lady," Lafitte said to the painting, "and if Azalee La Fontaine marries me, I will give it to her on our wedding night. It will look even more wonderful on her than it did on you."

Chapter 13

With Johnny and Lafitte both gone, Azalee had nothing to do but wander about the mansion, looking at the flowers and playing with the tropical birds. And she had time to think—too much time.

Madame Pompom had spoken of three men in her life, and, ever since they had rescued her from the *George,* she had been with two of them.

" . . . the three men . . . two will love you and leave you, one will pretend to love you, and one will return . . . " Those were Madame Pompom's words, and part of her prediction had already come true. Johnny Trent—he was the one who had pretended to love her and he had also left her. Madame Pompom said that one man would return—that certainly wouldn't be Johnny. Azalee remembered his words, *I wish I had never met you . . . I wish I had never met you.* She moved so abruptly that the birds took fright and flew high into the surrounding palm trees that decorated the conservatory.

"Mademoiselle," Yvonne whispered, interrupting

her thoughts, "a message has come for Captain Lafitte. I don't know what to do."

Azalee followed Yvonne into the huge kitchen, where an exhausted-looking man was wolfing down slices of buttered bread and drinking from a large bowl of coffee.

"What is it?" Azalee asked. "What's happened?"

"Captain Lafitte sent me out on watch—up north. I've been there for days, a week almost. It's just what the captain was afraid of. The British are going to attack New Orleans from the north. Everybody thought they would come in from the sea, but they're coming inland from the north. Somebody's got to get word to those soldiers in New Orleans. Somebody's got to tell them—"

"The New Orleans Regiment," Azalee said. "Finish your coffee—hurry—and ride for New Orleans."

The man shook his head and slumped in his chair. "I cannot, Mademoiselle . . . I'm worn out."

"There's no one here, Mademoiselle," Yvonne said. "Just a few of us in the house . . . everyone else is on patrol with Captain Lafitte."

"I'll go," Azalee said. "New Orleans is my home."

"By yourself, Mademoiselle?" Yvonne asked. "All alone? You don't even know the road—"

"I know the road," one of the men who helped in the kitchen spoke up. "Captain Lafitte says I'm too old to ship with him, but I'm not too old to ride."

"But, Marius," Yvonne said, "you don't even know how to ride."

"I used to ride," Marius said. "What do you think, Yvonne, that I was born at sea? I was born on a farm, north of New Orleans. I rode as a boy, and I can ride again."

"Have two horses saddled, Yvonne," Azalee said, "while I go up and change my clothes."

"But we don't have a sidesaddle," Yvonne said.

"I'll ride in Donaldson's clothes. See if you can find me boots, Yvonne—the smallest pair—and hurry."

Azalee and Marius mounted two of Jean Lafitte's horses. When Azalee saw how awkwardly the man moved in the saddle, she wondered if she wouldn't be better off going to New Orleans by herself.

"I'll be fine, Mademoiselle," Marius said, when he saw the expression of worry on her face. "It will just take me a little time to get used to the feel of the saddle—just a little time."

Azalee spurred her horse on. Marius jounced and bounced about in the saddle, but he managed to keep up with her.

Azalee, Marius, and the horses got some rest when they boarded the flat-bottomed skiffs that carried them across the patches of water that separated them from New Orleans.

Azalee was retracing her father's steps, when he had come to Barataria Bay, and, like her father, she would stare at the opposite shore, impatient with the slow-moving boat that carried them there.

"How much farther are we from New Orleans?"

she asked Marius every time they stopped riding and boarded another skiff.

"Not too much further. Mademoiselle, can we stop somewhere for the night? It's getting dark."

"You stop, Marius, at the next town. I'll go on without you."

"No, no," Marius said. "We'll go on together."

"We shouldn't have too much farther to go on horseback," Azalee said. "Where did you say we could get a boat for New Orleans?"

"At Pointe La Touraine," Marius told her. "We'll hire a boat and sail the rest of the way. I'll be happy to be on a ship again."

But when they arrived at Pointe La Touraine, Azalee had as much difficulty hiring a boat as her father had, when he tried to get to Grand Terre Island.

"New Orleans?" one captain said. "I have no business in New Orleans."

"Who are you?" another man asked Azalee. "You say your father will pay when we get to New Orleans, but how do I know that's true?"

"I'm Azalee La Fontaine. My father is Pierre La Fontaine," Azalee said impatiently.

The man laughed. "You expect me to believe that Monsieur La Fontaine's daughter goes around the countryside dressed like that? Money first, if you want to set foot on my ship."

"How much money?" Marius asked.

The captain named a price, and Marius reached into his shirt front and pulled out a brown leather pouch. He tugged at the drawstring and poured the contents into his hand. He held his hand out and Azalee saw extraordinary pearls. Each had a pale apricot luster and was as big as a large green pea.

Marius held one pearl up to the light. "This could buy you a new boat. And it's more than enough to pay for the young lady's trip."

The captain's eyes widened. "You have a fortune in pearls there, Monsieur. Not even Jean Lafitte has finer pearls than those."

"These are Jean Lafitte's pearls," Marius said, his voice hard, "and this lady is a special friend of Captain Lafitte's. I will give you one pearl for her passage, and should anything happen to her between here and New Orleans, it is Jean Lafitte you will answer to."

The captain took the pearl. "Nothing will happen. You have my word."

"And you have my word," Marius told him, "that Lafitte will come for you, if anything happens to Mademoiselle Azalee."

"Marius," Azalee said, "you're not coming to New Orleans?"

Marius shook his head. "I wouldn't be welcome. Some may remember me from when I sailed with Captain Lafitte."

"But there's an amnesty."

Marius grinned. "Maybe so, Mademoiselle, and maybe not. But, when I come to New Orleans, it will be with Captain Lafitte—safer that way."

More than once Azalee asked the captain if the ship couldn't go faster, and each time he said, "It's up to the wind. Not even another pearl could make this ship move faster.''

Wrapped in a cloak, she fell asleep in the middle of the night, and she awoke when the captain nudged her with his foot. "Here we are, New Orleans. Now I want to see how they welcome you, Pierre La Fontaine's daughter.''

Azalee rubbed her eyes and stood up. New Orleans. Was she really in her city? She moved quickly to the ship's rail and looked around. It was New Orleans. She had come home!

The captain watched her, as she walked down the gangplank and toward one of the three coaches that waited at the end of the dock. He watched as she spoke to the driver, and he saw the driver shake his head. No, of course not, the captain thought. No one would want to drive her anywhere. It was clear from the way she was dressed that the girl had no money.

He leaned over the railing, and he could see the girl take off the wide-brimmed planter's hat she had been wearing. He saw her shake loose a fall of very dark hair and then—then the coachman leaped down, calling out something to the other drivers, and helped the girl into the coach. The driver whipped up his horse, and that was the last the captain saw of the girl. But, by then, he knew what everyone up and down the length of the dock was saying.

"Did you see her?"

"It was Azalee La Fontaine!"

"Pierre La Fontaine's daughter. She's come back!"

"Azalee—did you see how she was dressed?"

So it was Azalee La Fontaine, after all. The captain reached into his pocket and took out the pearl once again. He turned it around in his hand. The man was right—it would buy him a new ship. But had he known she was really the La Fontaine girl, he would have demanded two pearls—and he would have gotten them, too!

Chapter 14

"BUT, MAMA, WHAT AZALEE DID WAS WONDER-ful," Alain said. "She saved the city."

"Wonderful," Madame Duval said, "just wonderful. A young girl living first on a British ship and then with a pirate!"

"None of that was her fault," Alain said.

"Nothing is ever Azalee's fault," his mother said sarcastically. "But the most extraordinary things seem to happen to her."

"If she hadn't warned us, New Orleans could have been destroyed. Nobody expected that the British would try attacking New Orleans from the north. They might have burned the city, just as they burned Washington."

"Admirable," Madame Duval said, "and, in time, perhaps the city fathers will erect a statue of Azalee. But this does not mean that I want a heroine in my family. Jeanne d'Arc was brave and wonderful, too, but I never heard that any mother wanted Jeanne d'Arc to marry her son."

"What's all this talk?" Theodore Duval asked. "Azalee is too young to marry, and Alain is still a soldier. Time to talk of this after the war."

"I don't want Alain to have the wrong ideas," Madame Duval said.

"I have no wrong ideas about Azalee," Alain said quietly. "All my ideas about her are right. You'll understand in time, Mama."

"I feel sorry for Charlotte," Madame Duval said, after Alain had left the house. "Imagine having a granddaughter with such a reputation!"

At the La Fontaine house, Nani Charlotte was echoing Madame Duval's sentiments. "Her life is ruined," she said to Pierre La Fontaine, "finished."

"Nonsense," Azalee's father said. "Aren't you proud of her? Azalee saved New Orleans. If she hadn't warned us, we wouldn't be sitting at this table enjoying our morning coffee. We would be hiding somewhere in the bayous."

"I just wish that warning could have come from someone else, Pierre. Who will want to marry Azie now? Did you see how she looked when she arrived in the city?"

"She couldn't have made the trip from Grand Terre Island in a ball gown. Believe me, I know what she went through to get here."

As Azalee came downstairs, she heard her father's last sentence. "And I know what you went through, Papa, when you went to Grand Terre Island. I only wish we could have been there together. Have you ever seen such beautiful things, Papa?"

"I didn't really notice Jean Lafitte's possessions," Pierre La Fontaine said stiffly.

"I don't mean the silver or the paintings," Azalee said. "I mean the birds and the flowers—"

"Azalee!" Nani Charlotte said, letting her butter knife fall against the plate. "I hope you will not talk about Jean Lafitte's house to anyone here in New Orleans. No descriptions of the birds and flowers, please! I'd rather that everyone forgot that you were ever at that pirate's house."

"That pirate saved me, Nani."

"Even so, no more talk about him, please. Sit down now and have your breakfast."

Azalee sat down obediently and said nothing more about Jean Lafitte, nor about anything else that was important to her. She was happy to be home, happy to see her father, Nani Charlotte, and Fanchon. But, as before, when she was with them, she had to pretend to be someone else. They loved her, but they wanted her to be different.

Would anyone ever accept her as she really was? she wondered. She had thought that Johnny Trent might be the man who would understand her yearning to be free and independent, but his words—*I wish I had never met you*—still stung. *But I was wrong, too. I should have told him how I really feel—I should have said, "Even if I never see you again, I'm not sorry that I met you. I'll always remember the way I felt when you held me in your arms for that one short dance. No man has ever made me feel that way, and no man ever will."*

"Azalee? Azalee!"

It was Nani Charlotte. She had been so far away with her thoughts of Johnny Trent, she hadn't heard what her grandmother was saying.

"Azalee, it's Alain Duval. He's in the garden. Now, Azie, please—please be nice to him."

Azalee knew what her grandmother meant. She meant: *Don't disgrace us again. Alain likes you. He may be your last chance to find happiness in New Orleans—the right kind of happiness. Try to say and do the right thing, Azalee.*

She looked at Nani Charlotte. She saw the pleading in her grandmother's eyes, and she knew that she was acting out of love for her. Azalee moved around the table and kissed her grandmother. "Don't worry, Nani. Everything is going to be all right. I promise."

Nani Charlotte sighed, and Azalee went into the garden.

"Azie . . ."

She held out her hand to Alain. He took it and drew her close to him. Azalee was surprised. Of all the young men she knew in New Orleans, Alain was the last one she would expect to behave so forwardly. She pulled back. Why had he tried to take her in his arms? Was it because he believed some of the stories circulating in New Orleans? *Azalee:* mistress to a pirate; *Azalee:* lover of an American Army officer; *Azalee:* heaven only knows what happened to her on that British warship!

She became stiff and rigid in Alain's arms, and he very gently let her go. "Forgive me," he said. "It's just that I'm so happy to see you—so relieved that nothing happened to you."

Azalee, still mindful of the whisperings of New Orleans, asked, "And what do you think might have happened to me, Alain?"

"You could have been killed," he said. "You were in a battle between the *Isabella* and the *George,* and then when Lafitte came in the *Corsair—*"

"There was no battle with Jean Lafitte," Azalee said. "He caught the British by surprise."

"Thank God for that," Alain said, "and bless that man for saving you."

Azalee thought she would cry. Alain was so good, so kind. He had no questions as to what she did on the *George,* or what had happened at Lafitte's mansion. He was just happy to find her alive. "Alain," she said, this time moving readily into his arms, "you're the best person I know, truly."

Alain didn't give her the passionate kiss that she would have been willing to accept at that moment. *Kiss me, Alain,* she wanted to say, *kiss me and make me forget Johnny Trent.* But his lips barely brushed hers, and, instead of holding her tightly, he stroked her hair.

The night of the ball. The night when she had danced with Johnny. She remembered how she had felt in his arms. She hadn't danced with Alain—maybe if she had, she would feel differently about him. "Alain, that night . . . we never even had one dance. It was my first ball, and you never asked me to dance."

"Oh, Azie." Alain thought she was about to bring up his dance with Felice, but he was wrong.

She moved toward him, her light morning gown floating about her, and she said, "Dance with me."

"When?" he asked. "Where?"

"Here," she said, "and now."

"But, Azie, we're in the garden. People may see us from the street—"

"Alain," she whispered, "please dance with me."

"There's no music," he said.

"I'll sing," she said softly. "I remember the melody of one of the waltzes they played that night. Alain," she held out her arms, "please."

He moved toward her, and she was in his arms. Roses brushed against them as they slowly waltzed among the flowers. Alain felt Azalee's delicious warmth as he held her. The music she hummed was faint and delicate in his ears, and his lips brushed her shining hair. "Azie," he whispered, "I love you so."

Azalee stopped dancing. Nothing. She had felt almost nothing when she was in Alain's arms. It was sweet, dancing with him, but that was all. Her heart didn't pound, her blood didn't race. But maybe it was better this way. Alain didn't make her feel the way Johnny had made her feel, but Alain would never say *I wish I had never met you.*

Try as she might, she couldn't say that she loved him. She did say, "You've always been so good to me, Alain. I think you're the kindest man I've ever known—the best. You're such a good friend."

Alain took her hands. "I want to be more than a friend to you, Azie. Don't you know that?"

"I . . . I'm not sure."

"I wanted to tell you the night of the ball, but your father said to wait. He said that you were too young."

"But that was some months ago, and I'm almost seventeen now," Azalee said with a smile. "I will be in a few months."

"That's why I don't want to wait any longer," Alain said. "I know your father doesn't want you to become engaged right now. But, Azie, there's a war on, and I must know. Will you wear my ring when you're seventeen?"

He's not the man, she thought, *he's not the man I want to marry.* But would she ever find a man that she did want? Johnny had left her, and she would never see him again.

Azalee turned her head slightly, and she saw her grandmother looking at her through the French doors that separated the morning room from the garden. Her grandmother was beseeching her. She could see that in her eyes. Her grandmother was telling her to accept Alain, to be grateful that he still loved her. She was begging her not to disgrace the La Fontaine name still farther.

She moved toward Alain, and he kissed her ever so gently. "Azie?"

"Yes, Alain," she whispered. "I'll wear your ring . . . when I'm seventeen."

"Oh, Azie," he said, hugging her, "you've made me

so happy. I've always loved you." And over his shoulder, Azalee saw her grandmother's relieved smile.

She wanted to say the right words to Alain, but she couldn't tell him that she loved him. She would become engaged to him, and, in time, she would marry him. She would settle down and be the kind of wife that Alain deserved, but she just couldn't say that she loved him—not yet, maybe never.

"I hope you're not too angry, Monsieur La Fontaine," Alain said to her father, when they walked back into the house. "I know you wanted me to wait, but with the war—everything is moving so quickly. I've asked Azalee if we could become engaged on her seventeenth birthday. I know I should have talked to you first, sir."

"It's all right, Alain," Nani Charlotte said, before her son could speak. "We've known you since you were a child. We know your family. Of course, we're delighted."

"Azie," Pierre La Fontaine said, taking his daughter tenderly in his arms, "is this really what you want?"

Azalee understood her father's unspoken question: *Do you really love Alain?* "Yes, Papa," she said, "this is what I want."

Alain took Azalee from her father's arms and, when he held her, Azalee felt much the same as she had when her father had held her. "I'm so happy," Alain said. "I've never been so happy in my whole life. I'll go home and tell my parents. Azie, let's have a party and tell everyone—"

"Alain, we're not yet engaged. And I'm not ready to face a whole lot of people."

"Why not?" Pierre La Fontaine asked his daughter sharply. "I've never known you to be afraid to face people, Azie."

And then, to everyone's surprise, Azalee threw herself down on a sofa and wept. "I know what everyone in New Orleans is saying—all that talk about what I did on the *George* and what I did at Jean Lafitte's home—I've heard them. When I've done nothing . . . nothing."

"Azie, Azie," Alain said softly, as he sat down and put his arm around her, "you did something wonderful. You saved New Orleans from a British attack. And I've never known you to care about what other people think."

"I never did," Azalee said, sobbing, "but now when I walk down the street people whisper. And some people turn away. I wish I were at Aunt Paulette's. I wish I could go there now."

"No," Pierre La Fontaine said, "I won't let you run away. You have done nothing to be ashamed of. I agree with Alain. We'll give a party! It won't be a grand one, because of the war, but a small party for our friends, to let them know that you and Alain will soon become engaged."

"Yes, Alain," Nani Charlotte concurred, "tell your parents how pleased we are and tell them that we plan to give a small party in honor of your coming engagement."

"But, Nani," Azalee said, "all those people—"

"Exactly, Azie. All those people. All our friends. If they *are* our friends, they'll be as happy as we are."

"You will tell your parents, Alain?" Pierre La Fontaine asked.

"I'll go right now. Azalee . . . I love you. I'll be back as soon as I can."

"I'll be waiting," Azalee said quietly, "thank you, Alain."

Chapter 15

"YOU CANNOT BE ENGAGED TO THAT GIRL," MADAME
Duval said.

"Not exactly engaged—just engaged-to-be-engaged.
We have to wait until Azalee is seventeen," Alain told
his mother.

"Even then—you cannot marry Azalee La Fontaine."

"I love her, Mother."

"You're young, Alain. You'll meet plenty of girls,
girls who are even prettier than Azalee."

"Maybe prettier," Alain said, "but no one with her
spirit, her bravery."

"Bravery! You call it brave to live with a pirate on
some secret island somewhere? Yes, I suppose you
could call a girl who lives with Jean Lafitte brave, but I
would call her a few other things, as well."

"Lafitte saved her from the British, Mother. What
was Azalee to do? She had to go to Grand Terre Island.
Where else could she have gone?"

"And I suppose she had to stay there, too. She was

there for several days, Alain. She didn't seem in a hurry to get back to her family."

"She couldn't get back. She had a fever and then there was no one to bring her back—"

"She got back easily enough when she wanted to."

"It wasn't that easy, and she made that journey because she had to warn us."

"I told you, Alain. I'm not interested in having a heroine for a daughter-in-law."

"And I've told you, Mother. Azalee makes me happy—happier than I've ever been."

Madame Duval sighed. She looked at her tall soldier son. Alain was very good-looking, and, in his red-jacketed uniform, she thought he looked even more handsome. She wanted to push a dark lock of his hair away from his forehead, but he was no longer a little boy. He had a mind of his own. She knew she had to agree to his engagement to Azalee. But they weren't married yet, and once the war was over, Alain would meet other girls, suitable girls—she would see to that. "Very well, my dear," she said, "if Azalee makes you happy, I won't try to stop you."

"The La Fontaines are planning to give a party for us—" Alain began.

"A party! I should think they'd be happy just to have Azalee back without creating any more of a fuss. Besides, no one would come to the party. New Orleans is too shocked by Azalee La Fontaine to go to a party in her honor."

"The party is for both of us, Mother. And everyone will come . . . if you do."

Madame Duval didn't want to attend a party that would celebrate her son's engagement to Azalee. But engagements could be broken, and she would make sure that this one was—once the war was over. Alain was her eldest son, and she would do anything to see him happy—even attend this farce of a party. "All right, Alain, all right! You and Azalee always have to have your own way. I will go to the party."

Alain smiled at his mother. "And one more thing . . . I'd like to give Azalee a ring."

"A ring! But I thought you weren't really engaged, that you were going to wait until Azalee is seventeen."

Alain nodded. "That's right. That's why I don't want a big ring—just that small emerald and diamond ring of great-grandmother's. It's so delicate, and the emerald matches Azie's eyes. I'd like to give it to her the night of the party."

Madame Duval shook her head. First she had to agree to her son's engagement to Azalee, then she had to promise to attend a party in their honor, and now she had to part with her grandmother's emerald ring. She had said *yes* to everything else, she might as well agree to this. "Very well, Alain. The emerald ring is yours."

"And Azalee's."

"And Azalee's," she echoed. "Is there anything else you'd like?"

Alain hugged his mother. "You're wonderful, Mother. I'm so happy."

That was the purpose of all her sacrifices, Madame Duval thought—to make Alain happy. But, when his engagement to Azalee ended, she'd be happy. Meanwhile, she would go along with what he wanted, though she couldn't really predict how the rest of New Orleans would react to the news of their engagement. Would anyone come to the party at the La Fontaine home? She couldn't guarantee it, no matter what Alain thought, but she would be there—she would do that for her son.

On the night of the party, Azalee faced her wardrobe filled with white dresses. She thought of the apricot silk and the lavender velvet she had left at Jean Lafitte's house, and she shut her eyes.

"The eggshell silk with the white embroidered lilies of the valley," Fanchon said. "My *petite* will look beautiful in that tonight."

Azalee shrugged. "Whatever you say, Fanchon."

Fanchon was worried. Was Azalee sick? She was quiet, so subdued. "It's time, Azie," Fanchon said. "Alain is waiting for you."

Azalee hid her face in her hands. "I don't want to go down," she said.

"My Azie? Not want to go to a party?"

"I'm not interested in parties anymore—parties are silly."

"Azie, are you ill? What's wrong?"

"I'm not just a spoiled child, Fanchon. Not just a silly girl who's only interested in parties." *Johnny,* Azalee was weeping within, *I wish you could see—I have changed.*

"Who said you were a spoiled child, *petite?* Who?"

"No one. All right, Fanchon, I'm ready. I'll go downstairs."

Fanchon watched Azalee walk slowly down the stairs. Was this her Azie? She used to caution her to move in a more ladylike way, but now she was too ladylike, too demure. Fanchon didn't like it. She wanted the old Azie back—the Azie who wore breeches, climbed the rigging, and dared to be happy. She had cautioned her about being too reckless, but reckless was better than this sad and quiet girl.

Alain was waiting for her at the foot of the stairs. "Azie, you're beautiful!" he said, as he gave her his arm.

They walked into the large salon where the guests had gathered. Azalee stood beside Alain and barely paid attention to her father, who made the ritual announcement: ". . . we are so happy . . . my daughter . . . Alain Duval . . . soon to be engaged . . . loving . . . young . . . happy you could all come . . ."

Alain bent to kiss her, and Azalee dutifully turned up her face. There, it was over. New Orleans would accept her again. She was soon to be engaged to Alain Duval.

But wait; something else was happening. What else could there be? Now Alain was speaking, and, again, she only caught fragments of what he was saying: ". . . my great-grandmother . . . her ring . . . my Azalee . . . until the engagement is official . . ." and the next thing Azalee knew, Alain was slipping an emerald ring on her finger.

The ring made her conscious of what had happened, of what she had promised to do. She had promised to marry Alain Duval, that's what all this was about. The ring made everything so final, so definite, but she didn't know if she wanted it to be that final, that definite. "Alain, a ring? But we're not really engaged," she said.

"My sweet, when we are engaged, I will get you a far finer ring than this one."

"Alain, this is a fine ring, but—"

"Azie," Alain whispered, so that none of the people coming to congratulate them could hear him, "wear it for me. It's just a small token of my love, but I want to think of you wearing it."

Alain was so sweet, so good. *He* didn't think she was a spoiled child. "Of course, I'll wear it. It's a beautiful ring, Alain."

The only one who had noticed Azalee's hesitation was Madame Duval. *She knows she's the wrong girl for Alain,* she thought. *She has enough decency left to know that she's not good enough for him. It won't be hard to end this engagement. Azalee will do it herself.*

"Well, now," Pierre La Fontaine said, as he came over to Azalee and Alain, "shouldn't we let these young people start the dancing? Alain?"

Alain turned to Azalee. "I never did have that waltz the night of the ball, but can we make up for it now, Azie?"

She moved obediently into his arms as the musicians played. The guests stepped back, and Alain and Azalee moved gracefully about the room. Azalee felt as though the smile on her face was painted on. Alain danced expertly, but without passion. He guided her easily, effortlessly, and was careful to keep his body a few inches apart from hers. As a dance it was perfect, but there was no suggestion of intimacy in the way they moved together.

After they had danced and were talking to some of the guests, Azalee saw a servant hurry to her father and whisper something to him. Pierre La Fontaine frowned and left the room. What could have happened? Azalee wondered.

The musicians continued playing, and some of the guests were dancing, while others were sipping champagne. Not too many people noticed when Pierre La Fontaine returned to the salon with the tall young man in the blue uniform of the United States Army.

But Azalee saw, and she turned away so that her back was to her father and the visitor.

Her father behaved as though Johnny Trent was just another invited guest. "Theodore," he said to Monsieur Duval, "you remember Lieutenant Trent?"

"Of course," Theodore Duval said, shaking Johnny's hand. "You're not bringing any pirates with you tonight, I hope?"

"No, sir," Johnny said. "I came to inquire after Miss Azalee. She did a brave thing, riding all the way from Grand Terre Island."

Theodore Duval was pleased. At least Azalee's ride to New Orleans was not caused by a desire for another meaningless adventure. Maybe she wouldn't make a bad wife for Alain, after all. "Lieutenant, this party is for Azalee and my son, Alain. They will become engaged very soon, when Azalee is seventeen. But that's just a formality—Alain just gave her his great-grandmother's ring. Let me take you to them. Alain will want to thank you for rescuing Azalee from the *George*."

Johnny felt as though his smile had frozen on his face. He didn't know if he could walk across the room to where Azalee stood with her back to him. Engaged, he thought. She was engaged. Well, what had he expected? She was engaged to a man who was right for her—right, the way he could never be—even though no man could love her more than he did. And before he could calm his stirred-up feelings, Johnny found himself looking down into her deep green eyes.

"Azalee, Alain, look who's here."

Azalee took a deep breath. "Lieutenant Trent, how nice to see you."

Now it was Johnny's turn to hold his breath—she was so lovely. "Azie . . . I mean, Mademoiselle . . . I was in New Orleans and I came by to see if you were all right."

She shrugged. "I'm fine, as you can see. Have you met my fiancé, Lieutenant?"

Fiancé. The word stabbed him like a knife, but he kept his smile frozen on. Johnny shook Alain's hand. "We've met before. You're a very lucky man, Lieutenant Duval."

Alain smiled and put a proprietary arm around Azalee. "This is the first time I've heard Azalee use the word *fiancé*—that tells me just how lucky I am."

Johnny looked into Azalee's emerald green eyes. "Is it all right to ask a newly engaged young lady to dance? I'd very much like to have one dance with Mademoiselle Azalee."

Alain smiled. "It's all right, Lieutenant, especially now that we both know that Azie can take care of herself—just like the girls from Tennessee."

Johnny looked at Alain, so resplendent in the dress uniform of his regiment, and remembered what he had said to him the first time they met. "I guess I said the wrong thing that night, Lieutenant Duval. It wasn't the first time, and it won't be the last. I tend to speak out of turn. Isn't that so, Mademoiselle?"

"I wouldn't know," Azalee said coolly. Johnny's smile was as unreal as her own, she noticed.

"Will you dance with me, Mademoiselle? I'll try not to talk too much."

"Of course," she said, and then she was in his arms.

This was it, she thought, as he pulled her close to him. This was the feeling she remembered, the feeling that only he gave her. Her hand was trembling in his, and he held her still closer. She felt as though she couldn't breathe. "Let me go," she whispered.

"Easy, easy," he said, "there's a whole bunch of

people looking this way. You don't want to give them anymore to talk about, do you?"

"How do you know people are talking about me?"

"Word gets around. I've been camped outside New Orleans for days. That's why I came tonight, Azie. I wanted to make things right. I wanted to let your father know that nothing happened at Grand Terre."

"My father doesn't need to hear that from you," Azalee said furiously. "My word is good enough for him."

"Smile, Azie," Johnny said, and she felt the pressure of his palm against the small of her back. "Everyone is looking at us, remember?"

"Then why won't you let me go?"

"Not just yet. Not until the music is over. I may not be from New Orleans, but even I know enough not to stop dancing until the music ends."

"The music *has* ended," Azalee said bitterly. "It ended for us that day on Grand Terre Island."

"Maybe I was wrong," Johnny said, his lips just brushing her hair. "Maybe I was wrong . . . a little. But I wasn't wrong all that much. You're doing the right thing, Azie. This is where you belong, and Lieutenant Duval is the right man for you."

Azalee struggled slightly, too conscious of the guests who watched them to do more. "I don't need you to tell me that," she said.

"I guess I'm not telling it to you," Johnny said, and she could hear the strain in his voice. "If I'm telling it to anybody, I'm telling it to myself. I've got to be sure that you're the wrong girl for me, or I'll go completely crazy. And you are the wrong girl for me, aren't you, Azie?"

"Completely wrong! I'm a spoiled child used to getting my own way. And I'm not about to change one little bit for you, Johnny Trent!"

"Glad you said that," he said, holding her so tightly that she almost cried out. "I needed to hear you say that. We're not for each other, Azie. Another time, another place, another life, maybe. But not now . . . we'd be all wrong together."

"Absolutely," Azalee said, "absolutely wrong."

Johnny took a deep breath. "Now the music has ended, Mademoiselle Azalee La Fontaine, and I want to thank you for the dance. I shall remember it for the rest of my life, because there won't be another."

He let go of her, and Azalee felt cold and tired. "You're right," she said softly, "we won't dance again . . . not ever again."

Chapter 16

IT WAS SETTLED. AZALEE KNEW WHAT SHE WOULD do. She would marry Alain after the war. She would be a proper wife, a proper mother, and she would never know the sweet wildness that she might have had with Johnny Trent.

But what could a proper young lady do in New Orleans with the war still going on? Azalee did exactly as her friends did—she volunteered for work at the local hospital and helped care for wounded soldiers.

Marguerite Brevard was still a loyal friend. She'd been working at the hospital for more than a month, and she did her best to make things easier for Azalee. "This is where the bandages are kept," she said, "and the medicines are here. You follow Doctor Villard on his morning rounds, take notes, and make sure that his orders are carried out."

"Mademoiselle La Fontaine won't be doing that just yet," Nurse Passy said. "She has a lot to learn first. Suppose you start in the kitchen, Mademoiselle, helping the cooks prepare breakfast and lunch for the men. And you can serve the meals, too."

Marguerite was shocked. "But none of the volunteers do that. Why can't Azalee do what the rest of us are doing?"

"Never mind, Marguerite," Azalee said, "I'll be glad to do anything I can."

It was clear that, while some people accepted her, to others she was still the La Fontaine girl with the scandalous reputation. If working in the hospital kitchen was all she had to do to make people forget her past, she would happily do it.

For the next few weeks, Azalee did whatever the senior nurse ordered her to do. She worked in the kitchen, served meals, and scrubbed floors.

One afternoon, she, Marguerite, and some of the other volunteers sat in the nurses' room having a much needed cup of coffee. They were all exhausted.

"Look at your hands, Azalee," Felice Duchamps said with obvious relish. "They're so red. And your nails, they're all broken."

Azalee held up her hands. Felice was right. They were in terrible shape. She looked at Felice and remembered the night of the Duval ball, the night Alain had danced with Felice, and she had first danced with Johnny Trent.

Felice was staring at her hands. "They do look terrible," she said. "And Alain's ring seems so out of place." Azalee said nothing, but all the other girls knew that Felice yearned to wear Alain's ring. "Poor Alain," Felice continued, "so kind, so good. Always willing to do things for his family and for his family's friends."

"You love Alain, don't you, Felice?" Azalee asked.

"That's not true," Felice said, blushing. "But he

gave you that ring to please your grandmother and his mother, because they're such good friends. Everyone knows that!"

Azalee laughed. She had a pretty good idea of how Madame Duval felt about her. "Madame Duval would have been much happier to see you with this ring, Felice," she told her. Azalee saw that Felice had tears in her eyes, and she felt terrible. She, too, knew what it was like to lose the man she loved. "I'm sorry, Felice," she said. "All this stupid talk about rings—"

"You don't have to be sorry for me, Azalee La Fontaine," Felice said angrily, as she got up from the table. "I don't need *your* pity."

But I need yours, Azalee thought. *If you only knew.*

"Don't pay attention to her, Azie," Marguerite said. "She's just jealous."

"It's more than that," Azalee said. "She's unhappy. She really does love Alain."

"Maybe she does," Marguerite said, "or maybe she just wants to marry into the Duval family."

Azalee shrugged. It was all so unimportant. Her friends were such children. Some of them were older than she was, but it took pain to make someone grow up. It was pain that made a person mature, she now knew, not the passing of months or years.

The next few weeks brought maturing changes to everyone. The British blockaded the city, and the people of New Orleans learned what it was to do without. At first, it was only a few luxuries—they ran out of their precious coffee, and then they were short of sugar. But, in a while, it wasn't just coffee and sugar that were missed. As the blockade continued, the city ran low on all food supplies.

"We will manage," the citizens of New Orleans told each other. "The American Army will come soon, and, with their help, the New Orleans Regiment will beat the British. Until then, we will manage."

But *until then* was a long time in coming, and soon they were wondering how they would manage for hospital supplies. The volunteers worked days and often nights.

One day Nurse Passy came up to Azalee. "You make the rounds with Doctor Villard," she said. "You understand just what it is the doctor wants done, Azalee, and you're the least likely to faint at the sight of blood."

A few days later, Marguerite said wearily, "Azie, do you realize it's almost Christmas? What kind of a Christmas are we going to have this year? I can't bear it. Christmas was always the best time in New Orleans, and look at us now."

"We'll do our best," Azalee said. "We'll have a party here in the hospital for the men."

"Here in the hospital? How can we? Look at some of the soldiers. We don't even have fresh bandages for them."

"I know," Azalee said, "that's just why we have to do something for Christmas. It's the least we can do."

That night, when she came home from the hospital, she spoke to her father. "We need wine, Papa, for the hospital."

"Wine? Have they completely run out of medicine, then?"

"No, no. I mean for a Christmas Eve party."

Pierre La Fontaine was disappointed in his daughter. "Azie, this is no time to be thinking of a party."

"You're wrong, Papa. This is *just* the time to be thinking of a party. We don't have enough bandages; we don't have enough medicine—we must do what we can on Christmas Eve."

Pierre La Fontaine was ashamed. "I will ask the others, Azie. We'll bring what we can to the hospital." He looked at his beautiful daughter and felt proud. "You're right, of course."

"We'll get dressed on Christmas Eve," Azalee told the other volunteers. "Arrange your hair, wear your jewels, put on your best dresses . . . "

"I'm too tired," one of the girls said. "After working in the hospital for eight hours, I don't feel like getting dressed as though I were going to a ball."

"*You're* tired?" Azalee said, taking the girl by the hand and pulling her to her feet. "Look out there." She opened a door that led to a ward full of wounded men. "Look at them! Tell me once again that you're tired."

"All right, Azalee, all right. I'll do my best, we all will."

And so it was that on Christmas Eve, in 1814, the people of New Orleans turned out for a party at the small hospital that housed the wounded soldiers who had done their best to protect the city.

There was wine—more wine than food. The ship-owners went into their wine cellars and brought up the best they had. And, if there wasn't enough food, there were pretty girls to keep the soldiers happy. Azalee and the other hospital volunteers put on their most elegant gowns and walked from bed to bed, serving the soldiers glasses of wine and giving them small presents.

"You're wonderful, Azie," Alain said. He had come off duty and had hurried to the hospital to see her. "A party in the middle of a war . . . only you could have done it."

"That's true. Only Mademoiselle Azalee could have arranged all this." Azalee and Alain looked at the man who was so enveloped in a cape that his face was hardly visible.

He opened his cape, swept off his hat, and there he was. "Captain Lafitte!" Azalee said.

"How did you get through?" Alain asked. "How did you get past the British blockade?"

Lafitte laughed. "We didn't get through the blockade—we got around it."

"We?" Azalee asked.

"Why, yes," he said, smiling, "some of my men . . . and Lieutenant Trent. We had to get word to General Jackson and work out some plans. We couldn't do that by remaining at sea. And it is Christmas Eve, after all . . ." He signaled to his men and they brought out a few boxes. "It's not much, but it's the best we could do."

Nurse Passy and some of the doctors opened the

boxes. "Bandages," Nurse Passy cried out, "and laudanum! If you only knew how much we need it."

One of the doctors opened a small box and pulled out something made of a silvery cloth. "But this. What's this?" he asked. "Some kind of bandage?"

Lafitte took the box from him. "This isn't for the hospital, it's for Mademoiselle Azalee. Merry Christmas, Mademoiselle."

Azalee lifted the silvery fabric from the box. It was a gown—the most beautiful gown she had ever seen. She looked at the dress, and then she very carefully folded it and put it back in its box. "Thank you, Captain Lafitte, but I can't accept it. After I left Grand Terre Island, I became engaged . . . well, almost . . . to Lieutenant Duval."

Lafitte's eyebrows went up. He looked at Alain and Azalee. "Ah. Almost? You did say *almost,* Mademoiselle?"

"We're waiting until I'm seventeen," she explained.

"And then?" he asked.

"And then we'll be officially engaged."

"But just engaged, not married?"

"There are many things to be arranged before a wedding, Captain," Azalee said. "The settlement, the dowry . . ."

"Of course, Mademoiselle," Lafitte said, "I understand. And that's why I would like you to accept this gown . . . in honor of your coming engagement."

"I don't think so," Alain said.

"And it is Christmas," Lafitte said to Alain. "If anyone in this hospital has a pleasant Christmas, it is because of Mademoiselle Azalee. Surely, she deserves a little pleasure in return."

Alain looked at Azalee. He had seen the way she had held the gown. "Thank you, Captain," he said. "I only want to please Azalee."

"Captain," Pierre La Fontaine said, offering Lafitte a glass of wine, "some Bordeaux?"

Jean Lafitte took the glass and sipped the wine. "Excellent," he said. "It's moments like this, Monsieur La Fontaine, that I'm glad I didn't capture every merchant ship that sailed in and out of New Orleans."

The man is outrageous, Pierre La Fontaine thought, openly admitting his piracy. But, then, it was this same outrageous man who just might break the blockade. "Come along, Captain," he said. "Monsieur Duval would like to talk to you. We would like to hear something of General Jackson's plans."

Lafitte was reluctant to leave Azalee. "Yes, the general's plans," he said. "And, after that, I want to talk to you again, Mademoiselle. Marius told me something of your brave ride from Grand Terre Island to New Orleans, but I would like to hear the whole story from your own lips."

"Of course, Captain Lafitte," Azalee said.

After Lafitte and Pierre La Fontaine had walked away, Alain said, "I don't want you spending too much time with that man, Azie."

The old, rebellious Azalee almost responded with, *I'll do what I please, Alain.* But all she said was, "Of course. Whatever you want."

Chapter 17

AFTER ALAIN LEFT THE HOSPITAL TO RETURN TO HIS regiment, Lafitte walked over to Azalee. "Are you really going to marry him, Azalee?" he asked.

Azalee. Jean Lafitte had always called her Mademoiselle. She looked at him. "Yes, Captain," she said, "I am going to marry Alain Duval."

"But you don't love him." Azalee didn't answer him. "And as long as you're going to marry someone you don't love, you might as well marry me. You'll have a much better time, if you do."

Azalee smiled. Why was it easier to talk to Jean Lafitte than to either Alain or Johnny Trent? she wondered. Maybe because there was no question of love on either side. "I don't think my family would be very happy if I married a pirate, Captain Lafitte," she told him.

"But I won't be a pirate forever," he said. "There's going to be a battle soon. Both Jackson and I are sure of it, and, if I help the Americans win, I'll be a respected citizen. Who knows? Maybe I'll even become an officer in the American Army. Would you like that, Azalee?"

She shrugged. "If I loved you, I wouldn't care, Captain Lafitte."

"No?" He looked at her over the rim of his wine glass. "Somehow, I thought you were partial to officers—particularly lieutenants. If I join the army, I assure you I'll be at least a captain. Marry me, Azalee. You'll have a more amusing time of it."

"Amusing? But what about love, Captain Lafitte? Alain loves me, but I don't think you do. So why ask me to marry you?"

"I didn't say I loved you, Azalee. But I do want you—not enough to spoil my plan to settle down and become a gentleman shipowner, of course. You see, I'm not the pirate you think I am. If I were, I would take you out of here, and, once I had you aboard my ship, there would be nothing anyone could do about it."

Azalee thought of Madame Pompom and smiled. "Someone once predicted that there would be a man in my life who would only pretend to love me," she told him, "and now I know who that man is."

"I could give you a wonderful life, Azalee. Money, jewels, excitement. And you could give me what I need: youth, beauty, and position. It would be a perfect match." Lafitte, seeing that he hadn't changed Azalee's feelings one bit, tried harder. "And if you do marry Alain Duval, you won't stay with him for long. He won't give you the excitement you need."

Azalee was smiling, but her eyes showed she was

firm. "Nevertheless," she said, "I'm going to marry Alain."

Lafitte shrugged. "Perhaps. But you won't stay married to him. I know that—and so do you, my pretty Azalee."

"Another prediction?"

He took her hand and brought it to his lips, his eyes on her the entire time. "And when you decide to leave Alain Duval, just remember. I'll be waiting for you, Azalee." She tried to pull her hand free, but Lafitte held it tightly, and she wanted no scene in the hospital, with half of New Orleans watching them. "Promise that you'll remember."

She knew he wouldn't release her hand until she said the words. "I promise, Captain Lafitte."

"Jean."

"Jean," Azalee repeated.

"What's all this?" Pierre La Fontaine asked, walking up to them. "What promise did you make to Captain Lafitte, Azalee?"

"Mademoiselle Azalee promised to visit Grand Terre Island—with Lieutenant Duval, of course."

"There will be no visits with the British blockading the port, Captain Lafitte."

"General Jackson has plans for the British, Monsieur La Fontaine," Lafitte said. "Lieutenant Trent will be here in a day or two to tell you about them."

Johnny Trent. Did that mean she would see him again? She was committed to Alain, and she wanted nothing more to do with Johnny or with Lafitte. She wanted a quiet life, as Madame Alain Duval, and, to prove it to herself, she started to wrap Lafitte's gift and return it to him.

Madame Duval came up to her. "That's a beautiful gown," she said, as she watched Azalee fold it into the box. "But do you think you should have accepted it from Captain Lafitte, Azalee?"

"I'm returning it, Madame Duval," Azalee told her. "Although Alain said it would be all right to accept it," she added defensively.

"Did he? But men are so innocent, aren't they, Azalee?"

Azalee stiffened. "I haven't done anything wrong, Madame Duval," she said. "Alain knows that."

"I know it, too," Alain's mother said, "but appearances count, Azalee."

"I'll make Alain a good wife," Azalee said. "He'll never regret marrying me."

Madame looked at her, and, for the first time since she returned to New Orleans, she felt warmth toward Azalee La Fontaine. "I really think you mean that, Azalee—"

"I do, really."

"But can you do it? Alain is a quiet boy, and you've become used to a more exciting life," she said, looking over to where Jean Lafitte stood talking to Pierre La Fontaine.

"I've had enough excitement, Madame Duval. I don't want any more."

"I hope that's true, Azalee. I don't want my son to be unhappy."

"I'd never make Alain unhappy," Azalee said with feeling. "I promise you that."

Madame Duval looked around her. She saw the young women of New Orleans, beautifully dressed, talking to the wounded men, and she saw her husband and others serving the soldiers wine and whatever food they had to offer. There was a war going on, but here there was still some vestige of gaiety and celebration on Christmas Eve.

"This was a good idea, Azalee, having a party here at the hospital. Maybe you have changed—maybe you are thinking more of other people than of yourself."

Azalee closed the box that held the silvery gown. "I am trying to be what Alain and you and my family want me to be, Madame Duval," she said.

Alain's mother nodded. She was pleased with Azalee. Everyone was pleased with Azalee—everyone but Azalee herself.

Could she live her life as a lie? Azalee wondered. If she married Alain, she would have to. She looked at Jean Lafitte talking to her father. He had said that she wouldn't be able to stay married to Alain, that her need for excitement would betray her. But she wouldn't let it, she would never hurt the one man who offered her a safe harbor for the rest of her life.

He had to see her, Johnny Trent decided, as he rode toward New Orleans. Ever since he had heard her use the word *fiancé*, he had been haunted by the fear of losing Azalee for good. He had to tell her that he was wrong, had always been wrong about her. The wild streak that he had seen in her the very first night they met was what he loved about her. Why had he wanted to change her? Why hadn't he trusted her—and trusted his own feelings of love for her?

Johnny spurred his horse to a gallop, and he heard the word *wrong, wrong, wrong* echoed in every hoof-beat. What difference did it make if she couldn't live in a place like Tennessee? He would live in New Orleans, he would live anywhere—as long as he could be with her.

It was late at night when Johnny arrived at the hospital. Azalee had just finished an eight-hour shift, but she was too tired to rush home. She sat alone in the small room that had been set aside for nurses and volunteers, and she was drinking a small cup of chicory-laden coffee. It was a bitter brew, but Azalee hoped it would give her enough strength to leave the hospital and get into the carriage her father had sent to take her home. At the moment, though, she was too tired to do anything but sip her coffee and sit perfectly still.

"Azalee." She heard the voice that held just a touch of a Tennessee drawl. He was the only person who sounded quite that way. She didn't have to turn her head to know that Johnny had come into the room. He came around to the other side of the table to face her. "They said I'd find you here."

"What do you want, Lieutenant?" she asked.

"I had to see you . . . had to talk to you."

He looked haggard and exhausted—every bit as

exhausted as she was. And he looked older, so much older than when she had last seen him. It was the war, she decided, it had to be.

"I don't think we have any more to talk about," she said. "We said everything the night of my engagement party."

Johnny sat down and faced her across the small table. "Is that coffee?" he asked. "I could use some. I've been riding all night."

Azalee pushed a cup across the table to him. She was too tired to pick up the coffeepot. "Help yourself," she said.

He watched, as she held her cup in both hands and took another sip of the bitter coffee. "Azalee La Fontaine drinking coffee made with chicory out of a big, old china cup," he said. "I always thought of you as porcelain, Azie, and I pictured you as sipping from a delicate porcelain cup, too."

Azalee slammed her coffee cup down on the table. "Have you ridden all night just to tell me again how spoiled and unsuitable I am, Lieutenant?"

"No," he said softly. "I've come to tell you that I'm all kinds of a fool. I was crazy the night of that party— crazy to think that I could ever let you marry anyone but me . . ."

"But I'm the wrong girl for you," Azalee said bitterly. "You said so yourself. We're not meant for each other. You told me to marry Alain Duval."

"I know what I said. You don't have to remind me."

"Then why did you come here?"

"Because I love you, Azalee. And because I know

you love me. And because you'll always belong to me."

Azalee buried her head in her hands and started to weep. "It's too late—don't you see that? It's too late . . . "

He came around to her side of the table and pulled her to her feet. She was in his arms, and she felt his kiss burning her lips. She was shaking so, if he hadn't been holding her, she would have fallen to the floor. She held onto him, and she felt herself returning his kiss.

"Now," he said, still holding her, "do you still think it's too late?"

"Yes," she said wearily, pulling herself from his arms, "much too late. I've given my word—to Alain, to my family. I've hurt them enough. I'll never do anything to hurt them again."

"What about your word to yourself?" he asked. "You know you love me. Doesn't that count for anything?"

"It might have, once—but not now. I can't think only of myself any more. I can't do what I want . . . "

Johnny put his arms around her and held her to him tenderly. "Did I call you spoiled? What happened to that spoiled child, Azalee?"

"I guess she grew up," Azalee whispered. "Now, let me go, Johnny. Please . . . let me go."

He did as she asked and they faced each other. "I'll always love you," he told her.

"And . . . and I'll always love you . . . "

Then he was gone.

Azalee put her fingers on her lips. She could still feel his kiss. She had done the right thing, she told herself, yet the pain she felt was almost unbearable. Is this what doing the right thing meant? Would she be in pain for the rest of her life?

A few days later, when Alain came to her, Azalee was glad that she had sent Johnny away.

"I only have an hour," Alain told her. "They've canceled all leaves, Azie. We received word that British ships are coming in force. There's going to be a battle; maybe the last one. We're ready. Now if those troops of General Jackson's would arrive—"

"Alain," Azalee said, hugging him, "I'm so afraid for you."

"Don't be," he said. "I'll be all right. I have to be. I have you to come back to." He held her gently. "Do you know, Azie, even though we're at war, these last few weeks have been the happiest of my life? You've promised to marry me, and, if anything should happen—"

"Alain—"

"Nothing will. But if . . . if something does happen, I will have had this . . . knowing that you love me, that you want to marry me."

"Oh, I do want to marry you, Alain," Azalee said, her heart full of gentle feeling for him. "I do. Come back to me."

Alain kissed her lightly on the lips. "Nothing can keep me from you, Azie," he said.

Azalee walked with Alain to the courtyard of the

hospital, and she stood at the wrought-iron gate, until he disappeared from sight. When she turned to go back inside, a figure moved from the shadows and came toward her.

"Bless you, Azalee," Madame Duval said, her eyes filled with tears. "Bless you. No matter what happens, you've made my son happy."

"Madame Duval. I didn't see you . . . "

"I just wanted one more glimpse of him—but the moment belonged to the two of you."

Azalee ran to Alain's mother. "He'll be all right, Madame Duval . . . he has to be."

The two women clung to each other, and then they heard it—the sound of guns booming across the water. The British were shelling New Orleans.

Chapter 18

IT WAS AN UNUSUALLY COLD JANUARY, THAT WINTER of 1815, and New Orleans was in a state of siege.

Azalee didn't know what a siege meant, until the British appeared in the New Orleans harbor and began shelling the city. Then she understood.

"Azalee . . . over here, bandages." She ran to a stretcher where a woman lay, her leg shattered at the knee.

"Water, nurse . . . water, please . . . " a voice called out to her.

Azalee ran for a pitcher and a glass, and she held the soldier's head in her lap, while he took a few sips. His uniform was bloodied, but she could see that he was wearing the jacket of the New Orleans Regiment. "The regiment," she said, "you're part of the regiment. Have you seen Alain Duval? Gerard Duval?"

The man shook his head. "Tried to hold the city . . . but they kept forcing us back . . . street by street. The British . . . they just kept coming. General Jackson, he promised . . . "

Where is General Jackson? That was the question in

the hospital and on the streets, as people ran from the guns, from the British troops.

"Azalee," Doctor Villard was saying, "I'm going out there. Put bandages, medicines in my bag. I've got to help them."

"I'm going with you."

They walked out of the hospital into the courtyard crowded with stretchers and out to the street. They were met by people running in the opposite direction. "Don't go that way," a man yelled. "The British . . . "

"Azalee," Doctor Villard shouted to make himself heard above the gunfire, "go back!"

"No," she shouted back at him, "I'm coming with you."

He took her by the hand, and they ran down the streets, clinging to walls when they could hope to avoid the shells, as they tried to get close to the harbor.

"Get down," Captain Corday shouted, when they turned the corner into a square still held by the New Orleans Regiment. "For God's sake, get down!"

Doctor Villard and Azalee bent almost double as Captain Corday approached them. "You got through, Doctor," he said. "Thank God."

Azalee followed Doctor Villard from man to man, handing him bandages, medicine, even holding a man's head in her lap, while the doctor did his best to bandage a mangled arm. Her dress and her hands were bloodied, but by now she was used to the blood. As they worked, she looked about her. Where is he? Where is Alain?

Suddenly, it was quiet in the square—a quiet that was more terrible than the noise of the cannon. The silence lasted only a minute, and then Azalee heard a different sound: a drumbeat, an ominous drumbeat! Steady, constant, and relentless.

"They're coming," a wounded man whispered. "The British."

Azalee stood up and looked toward the port. The smoke had cleared and she could see the line of ships—British ships—blocking the harbor. They were moving closer and closer, until they butted up against the docks. And coming down the gangplanks of the ships, marching in rhythm to the beat of the drums, came British troops: line after line of men wearing bright red coats, each carrying a rifle, with their bayonets ready.

Her heart began to pound. There were so many of them. How could they have ever thought that their one regiment could hold back an army like that?

The British troops marched off the ships and formed even lines. For a crazy moment, they reminded Azalee of toy soldiers; they moved so smartly, so perfectly.

But then, something strange happened to the perfect line of toy soldiers. All she could hear were the drums, but she could see that one, and then another, and then still another man fell in the ranks where they stood. The drumming stopped and Azalee heard rifle shots. She couldn't see where the shots were coming from, but she did see the first line of British troops fire their rifles in return.

More and more British were falling, to be replaced

by still more soldiers filing from the ships. And that's when she saw them—the riflemen of Andy Jackson's American Army! They weren't in smart uniforms like the British or like the New Orleans Regiment. Some men wore blue coats; others had on fringed leather jackets. But no matter what they wore, they were holding that endless line of British soldiers back!

"Those hats," Azalee said, laughing and crying at the same time. "Those wonderful men . . . and look at those hats . . . "

"Coonskin caps," Doctor Villard said, smiling. "That's what they call them. They're hunters, those men. Look, Azalee. The British . . . they're turning back!"

"No," Captain Corday said, "not yet. But the Americans are stopping them—the men in blue are pinning them down."

The men in blue, Azalee thought. *And where is Johnny?*

"How long can they hold them?" the doctor was asking Captain Corday. "There are so many British. Why didn't Jackson send more men?"

"Look!" Azalee shouted.

Captain Corday and Doctor Villard looked in the direction Azalee was pointing. Coming up behind the British ships, sailing directly toward them, their guns flashing red, were the ships of Jean Lafitte.

Azalee saw the tall masts of some of the British fleet crack and crumple to the decks below. Other ships were hit broadside and began to list into the water.

The lines of British soldiers were hastily ordered

back and they retreated, still firing. The blue-coated soldiers moved steadily forward, and the men of both armies met at bayonet point.

"They're trapped," Captain Corday shouted, a broad smile on his face, "between Lafitte and the Americans. They're trapped! We've won!"

"We have work to do," Doctor Villard said abruptly. "There's the wounded. We're far from finished. Azalee, I need your help."

"Yes, Doctor," she said, and she knelt beside him, while he worked on another soldier. Her face was smudged, and there were dark shadows under her eyes, but she did her best to return the soldier's smile.

"We've won, haven't we?" the soldier asked her. "All my friends, who died . . . " a sob came from the man's throat. "It was worthwhile, wasn't it?"

Azalee managed to keep herself from crying, but she couldn't stop her voice from trembling. "I don't know. I suppose it was worthwhile. I just don't know."

She still didn't know what had happened to Alain—or to Johnny. Only when she found that out would she be able to say whether it was worthwhile or not to her.

Chapter 19

"BLACK AGAIN, *chérie?* WHY MUST YOU ALWAYS wear black?" Fanchon tugged at Azalee's black silk skirt. "You have so many beautiful dresses—white dresses—right for a young girl. Yet you always wear black."

"You know why I wear black, Fanchon."

"For Monsieur Alain, of course. But he wouldn't want you to wear black all the time. He loved you too much for that."

"I am going with the Duvals to the parade and then to the reception for General Jackson," Azalee said. "Madame Duval will be wearing black."

"Madame Duval is poor Monsieur Alain's mother. She is in mourning for her son—"

"And I am in mourning for my fiancé."

"One can mourn in white dresses, too, *cherié.* Must you meet General Jackson dressed like an old crow? You are young."

"I don't feel young, Fanchon," Azalee said. "Too much has happened."

"I know, Azie, but it will pass. You will see, in time it will pass."

"Never," Azalee said. "Never!"

Fanchon sighed. "Go then, Azie, but you look more like a widow than a fiancée, and you were never even his bride."

"And I will never be anyone else's either," Azalee said firmly.

Azalee rode in her father's carriage to the Duvals'. She would stand with them and with the other families who had men in the New Orleans Regiment, while what was left of the regiment paraded before General Jackson. Her father and Nani Charlotte planned to meet her at the reception that would follow.

"Azalee," Madame Duval said, when they arrived at the Place d'Armes. "Stand here, beside me."

Ever since the night they had met at the hospital, Madame Duval treated Azalee as though she were her own daughter. Azalee had made Alain happy. He had died happy, and whatever she might have done before was now forgotten.

Azalee heard a military march. Then she saw General Jackson, accompanied by some of his officers, ride into the Place d'Armes. She looked straight ahead. She knew that Johnny Trent was riding beside the general, but, ever since she had learned that Alain had been killed in action, she had refused to see the blue-coated soldier. She would be as loyal to Alain in death as she had planned to be had he lived.

After the general took his place in the reviewing

stand, the New Orleans Regiment marched in review. The Place d'Armes was quiet. There was no music and no one spoke. Close to half of the regiment had been killed, and there was not a family who stood there who hadn't suffered a loss.

"Alain," Madame Duval said, trying to stifle a sob, "Alain . . ."

"Look, Madame Duval," Azalee said, holding the older woman's hand. "You see . . . in the third row. It's Gerard."

"Yes, Gerard," Madame Duval said. She dried her tears with a black-bordered handkerchief. "Thank God, there's Gerard."

After the parade, Andy Jackson stepped forward to congratulate the men who were receiving medals for exceptional bravery. Azalee couldn't help smiling when she saw Jean Lafitte standing before the American general.

The pirate captain had his wish. He was a pirate no longer, but an honored citizen who had helped save the day at the Battle of New Orleans. Azalee couldn't hear what the general was saying, but she saw him pin a medal on Jean Lafitte's coat and then shake his hand.

"That pirate," Madame Duval whispered.

"Not anymore," Monsieur Duval said. "Soon all of New Orleans will be receiving him in their homes."

"Never," Madame Duval said. *"Never!"*

But later, at the reception for General Jackson, Azalee saw that Madame Duval was as polite to Captain Lafitte as she was to everyone else.

Azalee was moving down the receiving line with her

father and her grandmother, when she came face to face with General Jackson. She looked only at him, trying her best not to glance at the man who stood so easily at his side.

"Well, now," the general said, taking Azalee's hand, "is this the young lady you've been telling me about, Lieutenant Trent?"

Johnny looked at Azalee and smiled. He had told the general about her—told him that he was determined to make her his wife. Now she stood before him, so serious in her black dress, and so sad. He longed to take her in his arms right then and there, to make the sadness disappear from her beautiful face. But, at that moment, all he could do was to present her formally to the general. "Yes, sir," he said. "May I present Mademoiselle Azalee La Fontaine, her father, Pierre La Fontaine, and her grandmother, Madame La Fontaine."

General Jackson smiled at them all, but he held onto Azalee's hand. "I hear you did a brave thing, young lady," he said, "riding all the way from Barataria Bay."

"Yes, sir, but—"

"No buts about it," Andy Jackson said. "You saved the city that time from a surprise British attack. Lieutenant Trent," he said, turning to him, "how come we didn't arrange for this young lady to receive a medal?"

"I'm sorry, sir," Johnny said. "I should have thought of it."

"You certainly should have! That's the trouble with squirrel shooters from Tennessee, Ma'am. Sometimes they don't know how they're supposed to treat a lady. But give this one time. He'll learn."

"I'm sure he will, sir," Azalee said, "and some young lady in Tennessee will be very happy about it."

"Young lady in Tennessee?" The general's eyebrows went up. "Lieutenant Trent, I thought you gave me to understand—"

"Yes, sir," Johnny said, "and now, there are some others who are waiting to meet you, sir."

General Jackson let go of Azalee's hand reluctantly. "I'd like to talk to you some more, young lady. Maybe you'll give me a minute after I say hello to all these folks here?"

"Yes, General, certainly," Azalee said, and she moved down the reception line without another glance at Johnny Trent. She didn't have to look at him. His face was burned in her heart and mind and would remain there forever. He looked wonderful in his dress uniform, but, once again, she thought he looked older than he did when they first met, which seemed so very long ago.

"Azalee," her father said, "were you polite to the general's aide? I'm not so sure—"

"Yes, Papa, quite polite. Please don't worry."

"Mademoiselle Azalee is always polite," Jean Lafitte said, as he came up behind them. "Your daughter has perfect manners, Monsieur La Fontaine."

"As do you, sir," Pierre La Fontaine said. "Azie, Nani and I must speak to the Duvals."

"Go ahead, Papa. I want to congratulate Captain Lafitte."

Jean Lafitte was silent, until they moved away. Then he said, "Well, Azalee?"

"Well, Captain Lafitte?" she answered.

"My offer still stands. I understand that your young man was killed at the Battle of New Orleans. I'm sorry about that, but—"

"But?" she interrupted him.

"But life goes on. And now your life can go on alongside mine."

"No, Captain Lafitte."

He frowned. "But, why not? I told you that my pirate days would be over, and they are. I told you that I would be accepted by New Orleans society, and I am. I am rich—what more do you want?"

"You don't love me, Captain Lafitte."

"Ah, yes, love—"

"And more important . . . I don't love you."

"You're still a child, after all," he said. "You want the moon. It's really too bad for you, Azie, to turn me down."

"Why too bad?"

"Because," Lafitte said after a moment, "I don't know how long I can remain an honest man without you by my side."

Azalee laughed. "Would I have made such a difference?" she asked.

"Of course," Lafitte told her. "You would have provided the excitement that I must have. Think about it, Azie. Without you, I might return to my old, bad ways."

"I don't believe that," she said, laughing. "You've

worked too hard to become a gentleman of New Orleans. I can't believe you'd give it up."

"Even a gentleman needs one special lady by his side, and you would have added a special grace and beauty to Grand Terre Island. Now, when the nights get lonely, I just may have to sail once again, looking for a little amusement."

"Please don't do that, Captain," Azalee said.

"Why not?"

"Because I like you," she said, "and I wouldn't like to think of you as a pirate again. I understand the authorities do terrible things to pirates if they catch them."

"Not to me," Lafitte said. "Do you see this medal? The general himself pinned it on, and the general himself granted me and all my men amnesty. I'm quite safe."

"Until you board the *Corsair* and go hunting."

Lafitte took Azalee's hand and bowed over it. "If I go hunting, I will think of you, Azalee. I will also think of you when I'm on my island." He let go of her hand, reached into his pocket, and brought out a velvet box. "I understand that you should have received a medal; I have brought you something to take its place."

Lafitte placed the box in her hands. Would she recognize the necklace? he wondered. She had seen it in the portrait of the lady in red.

Azalee didn't open the box. Instead, she tried to give it back to him. "I can't accept any gifts from you, Captain Lafitte," she told him.

"Nonsense," he said. "I had it made especially for

you. It was to be an engagement gift, if you had accepted me."

She opened the box and saw a diamond necklace glittering in the light of the candles. The necklace looked strangely familiar, but she didn't know why. She knew she had never seen it before. She closed the box and offered it to him. "No, Captain Lafitte, I cannot accept this."

He put his hands behind his back. "But I had it made for you. Keep it, Azie. Even if you don't wear it, keep it. If not, it's likely to go down to the bottom of the sea with me someday, and that would be a terrible waste. Besides, I would like to think that, even if you never wear it, you will pass it on to your daughter—another beautiful Azalee. And you will tell her about the pirate captain who gave it to you."

"No," Azalee said, "I will never marry, never have children. That part of my life is over."

Lafitte laughed. "Sometimes I forget how young you really are, Azalee. Well, then, keep it as a souvenir from Jean Lafitte. *Au 'voir,* lovely Azalee."

Chapter 20

"AZALEE," MARGUERITE SAID, "WE HAVE SOME-
thing to tell you."

Marguerite and Gerard had come to the La Fontaine
home to have afternoon coffee with Azalee. It was
almost like the old days, Azalee thought, except that
now there were just the three of them.

Azalee smiled. Marguerite and Gerard were sitting
close together on the carved rosewood couch, holding
hands. She knew what they were going to say, but she
decided to let them have the pleasure of saying it.
"Yes? What is it?"

Marguerite blushed as Gerard spoke. "We plan to
become engaged. We wanted you to know before
anyone else, because the four . . . well . . . the three of
us have always been so close, and there's no one we
love more than you, Azie."

Azalee hugged them both. "I'm so happy. Madame
Pompom's prediction really came true for you both,
didn't it? She said that Marguerite would have one
love, one man, and one marriage. That's clearly you,
Gerard."

"Yes," Gerard said, "and she said that I would know danger and sadness, but, after that, everything would be all right for me." He smiled at Marguerite. "It's a lot better than all right, now that I have Marguerite."

"I wonder what she saw in Alain's hand," Marguerite said. "Remember? She said she saw nothing. Do you believe that?"

"No," Azalee said. "I believe she saw his death in his hand. She just didn't want to tell him."

"She was right about all of us, then," Gerard said sadly. "All of us except Azie."

There were tears in Marguerite's eyes. "Azie," she said, "I'm so sorry. But in time—"

"No," Azalee said, pulling away from her friend, "no, never."

Marguerite dabbed at her eyes with a lace handkerchief. "Azie," she said, "when Gerard and I get married, will you be my maid-of-honor?"

"I'd love to, but what about your parents? Will it be all right with them?"

"All right?" Gerard said. "Azie, after what General Jackson said, everyone in New Orleans knows that you're a real heroine. Marguerite's parents would be delighted, and you know how much my mother loves you. My father, too."

Azalee sighed. New Orleans had accepted her once again. Now that it no longer mattered, all the whispering about her had stopped.

"Azie," Fanchon said, as she walked into the salon, "you have another visitor."

Johnny Trent was just a step behind Fanchon. "Azalee—" he began, and then he saw Gerard and Marguerite. "I'm sorry . . . I thought you were alone."

"We were just leaving," Marguerite said. "Gerard?"

"No, please," Azalee said, "don't go."

Gerard edged out the door with Marguerite. "We really must, Azie," he said. "We promised my mother to be back early."

"You shouldn't have come, Johnny," Azalee said bleakly, after her friends had left. "There's nothing for you here."

"There's you, Azie, and there's the way we feel about each other."

"But I don't want to feel anything anymore. I'd rather feel nothing than feel so much pain."

"Azie . . ." Johnny tried to take her in his arms, but she backed away from him.

"No," she said, "I can't. There's Alain to think of."

"Alain is dead," Johnny said. "You can't spend your whole life in mourning."

Azalee was weeping. "Yes, I can," she said. "That's what I want to do. I owe him that. He was so good . . . and I never even loved him."

"Azie, listen to me!"

"I don't want to listen to you . . . it's too late to listen to you! Go away, Johnny, please—please, go away."

He stared at her somberly. "I'm going . . . I'm

going. But I'll be back, Azalee. No matter how many times you send me away, I'll always come back."

The next morning at breakfast, Nani Charlotte poured Azalee a cup of coffee and said, "Did you know that that nice young aide of General Jackson's has become a captain, Azie?"

"Nice young aide? When did you decide that he was nice, Nani? I thought New Orleans didn't want anything to do with those 'crude backwoodsmen' of General Jackson's."

"New Orleans has changed," her grandmother said. "We're moving right along with the times, Azie. After all, we're part of the United States of America now, and there are all kinds of people out there. Not all of them are from New Orleans."

"I never thought I'd hear you say that, Nani," Azalee said.

"Neither did I," said Pierre La Fontaine, "but it makes a lot of sense."

Azalee finished her coffee quickly and left the table. She was spending more and more time alone, and, when she was invited to a party or an afternoon of coffee, she usually stayed at home.

She still enjoyed riding, but she preferred going out alone, and she took the paths out of the city, where she was least likely to run into any other riders.

One afternoon, Azalee turned Cinderella's head toward the bayou country. She wouldn't go as far as Madame Pompom's, but she rode in that direction, remembering the four lighthearted people who had ridden the same road not so many months before.

She kept Cinderella at a trot, and she was surprised to hear the sound of another horse behind her. She looked back, but saw no one, and she clicked her tongue to Cinderella, who quickened her step. The pace behind her also quickened, but, once again, when she looked back, there was no one there.

She remembered Alain telling her about the ghost of a pirate who haunted the bayous. Jacques Normand, that was his name. Was she being haunted by Jacques Normand?

Ridiculous! Her booted heels touched Cinderella's flanks, and the horse moved into a canter. Azalee listened. Yes, there it was, the rider behind her was still keeping pace with her. She couldn't move Cinderella into a gallop, because of the way the path curved among the swamps, but she could stop, and that was what she finally did.

She turned Cinderella around and rode back the way she came. She didn't like being followed and she decided it was better to face whoever—or whatever— it was than to try to run away. The other rider kept on coming, probably thinking that Azalee was moving on. When she rounded a curve in the road, they came face to face. It was Johnny Trent.

"You!" Azalee said. "I think I'd rather see Jacques Normand."

"Jacques Normand?"

"A ghost," Azalee said impatiently. "A pirate's

ghost—an old legend. Never mind. What are you doing here?"

"I followed you, Azie. I wasn't getting through to you back in New Orleans. I thought maybe out here in the open we could talk."

"We have nothing to talk about."

"We have *everything* to talk about—our whole lives together—"

"Not together, Johnny . . . never together." Azalee turned her horse around and headed down the path once more. "Go back to town, Johnny," she called over her shoulder. "I don't want to talk to you."

"But I want to talk to you," he said, and he spurred his horse so that he rode by her side. "You can't keep running away like this, Azie. Get off that horse," he said, reaching for her reins. "Let's talk."

"No," Azalee said angrily, reining her horse back from his. "I don't want to talk to you. Go away."

He spurred his horse closer to hers. "Get off that horse, Azalee, I'm losing patience."

"You're losing patience?" Azalee said furiously. "How dare you talk that way to me!" She spurred Cinderella who neighed, reared, and bolted down the twisting path at a gallop.

"Azalee," Johnny shouted, "come back here!"

But Azalee had no intention of coming back, and she spurred Cinderella on. The gray mare was willing, but the path was treacherous, and a few moments later, Cinderella tripped over an exposed tree root. Azalee couldn't keep her balance and fell off the horse.

"You're a little fool, after all," Johnny said, as he leaped off his horse and knelt beside her, "but I like you this way. Mad and sassy is more your style than sad and dignified. Are you hurt, Azie?" He felt her arms and shoulders. "Any broken bones?" he asked.

"Let go of me," Azalee said. "I'm fine . . . don't touch me. I can't believe it . . . I've never fallen off a horse before."

Johnny grinned and help her to stand and lean against a tree. "It's just your pride that's hurt, is that it? Your first time falling off? There's got to be a first time for everything."

"Not for me," Azalee said. She tried to move around him, but her back was against the tree, and he stood before her. "Get out of my way, Johnny."

"Not just yet," he said, and he leaned down and kissed her.

She had been trying to avoid that kiss—trying to avoid the way he made her feel—but then he kissed her again, and this time she didn't try to escape the touch of his mouth on hers.

He stepped back and looked at her. "Now tell me if you still want me to go away, Azie. But if you say it, be sure that you mean it. I wouldn't mind if you tell me to wait, but if you tell me to go, I will . . . and this time I won't come back."

"Don't go," Azalee whispered, and she took a step closer to him. "I don't want you to go . . . "

She was in his arms then, and she knew that her reckless heart had found a home, at last.

AFTERWORD
A Historical Note

Reckless Heart takes place in New Orleans, which was the capital of the French colony of Louisiana. Louisiana was transferred to Spain in 1762, returned briefly to French hands, and was then part of the Louisiana Purchase by the United States in 1803. The Creole background of many New Orleans citizens is a combination of their French and Spanish heritage.

The Battle of New Orleans, which is the historical climax of *Reckless Heart,* was also the climax of the War of 1812. General Andrew Jackson, who later became the seventh president of the United States, won a decisive victory at New Orleans against a well-trained British force led by General Edward Pakenham.

General Jackson had many sharpshooters from Tennessee in his army, and he was further helped by the pirate captain Jean Lafitte, who had refused a large monetary offer from the British and had fought on the American side.

Andrew Jackson and Jean Lafitte are historical characters, and the fictitious characters of Azalee, Johnny Trent, and the others are based on the people of that time, many of whom fought and died at the Battle of New Orleans.

Whatever became of Jean Lafitte? After a while, he went back to being a pirate, operating off the coast of Texas. As Azalee had predicted, he was, in time, captured by an American naval force, but he was also released—his service at New Orleans not forgotten. Captain Lafitte sailed away on one of his ships with some of his men. No one knows what finally happened to him or how he died. Does his ghost ship still sail in Barataria Bay? Legend says it does.

Dee Austin

STILL GOING STRONG!

First Love from Silhouette

BLOSSOM VALLEY BOOKS
by
ELAINE HARPER

plus

in response to those of you who
asked, whatever happened to
Janine and Craig after they
married?

First Love from Silhouette

First Love from Silhouette

THE MOST POPULAR TEEN ROMANCES PUBLISHED TODAY

The books that you have enjoyed
all these years with characters so real
they seem like friends,
and stories so engrossing that you have
begged for more!

4 TITLES A MONTH

Stories that mirror your hopes,
your dreams, your relationships —
the books that you have claimed
as your own ever since we first
published them.

AT YOUR FAVORITE BOOKSTORE

First Love from Silhouette

Is sixteen too young to feel the . . .

Romance, excitement, adventure—this is the combination that makes *Dawn of Love* books so special, that sets them apart from other romances.

Each book in this new series is a page-turning story set against the most tumultuous times in America's past—when the country was as fresh and independent as its daring, young sixteen-year-old heroines.

Dawn of Love is romance at its best, written to capture your interest and imagination, and guaranteed to sweep you into high adventure with love stories you will never forget.

Here is a glimpse of the first six *Dawn of Love* books.

#1 RECKLESS HEART
Dee Austin

The time is 1812, and wild and beautiful Azalee la Fontaine, the sixteen-year-old daughter of a wealthy New Orleans shipowner, is used to getting her own way. There's a war with England going on, and Azalee is warned to curb her reckless ways, but her daring and scandalous behavior makes her a prisoner in more ways than one. While the pirate captain Jean Lafitte can save her from one danger, only Johnny Trent—Azalee's fiery young man in blue—can tame her heart.

Read on . . .

#2 WILD PRAIRIE SKY
Cheri Michaels

The time is the 1840s; the place is the wagon trail west to Oregon. Headstrong Betsy Monroe knows she can meet any danger the trail offers. But Indians, raging rivers, and stampeding buffalo are the least of her worries. There's also Charlie Reynolds, the handsome young trail guide whose irresistible grin means nothing but trouble. When fate throws Betsy and Charlie together only two things can happen: all-out war or a love strong enough to shake the mountains.

#3 SAVAGE SPIRIT
Meg Cameron

The Kentucky frontier of 1780 is a wild place, as Catherine "Cat" Brant finds out when she is captured by Shawnee Indians and carried hundreds of miles from her home. Living in the Indians' village, she falls passionately in love with Blue Quail, a white captive who has been with the Shawnee so long he considers himself one of them. Can Cat make Blue Quail love her enough to leave the Indians and go back to her world?

#4 FEARLESS LOVE
Stephanie Andrews

It is hard to find time for romance during the 1836 Texan War for Independence from Mexico, but fiercely independent sixteen-year-old Lucy Bonner manages to share a few stolen minutes of love with Jesse Lee Powell, a crack young Tennessee rifleman. Lucy risks everything when she tries to save Jesse Lee and the other men of the Alamo and comes face-to-face with the Mexican Army and General Santa Anna himself!

Read on . . .

#5 DEFIANT DREAMS
Cheri Michaels

The War Between the States? Beautiful Savannah McLairn doesn't want to hear about it. This sixteen-year-old southern belle is not going to let the Civil War ruin what she calls her "prime party years." But swept along by the tides of change, Savannah finds herself behind Union lines, very much in danger of losing her rebel heart to a handsome, young Yankee soldier.

#6 PROMISE FOREVER
Dee Austin

Yearning for more love and excitement than she can find in 1840 New Bedford, Massachusetts, Tabitha Walker stows away on a clipper ship sailing for California. Once there, Tabitha finds more excitement than she bargained for. She also finds that she must choose between the two young men who claim her love: Alexi, the Russian aristocrat who can give her the world; and Tom Howard, the American sailor who can only offer himself!

Look for DAWN OF LOVE historical romances at your local bookstore!